Victoria

Book 17

Angel Creek Christmas Brides

ABOUT THE BOOK

Five years after the end of the Civil War, Victoria Montgomery has lost everything in her life that mattered. Her parents, her home, security, her freedom, and all hope of ever being happy again. Despite her reservations, she decides to honor the arrangement made by her father to marry a man he chose in Montana Territory.

What could make her life worse than it is? Living landlocked with a man who will never understand her independent ways.

Chance Turner retired his commission with the Union army and settled on a small ranch near the small town of Angel Creek. While many of the men in Angel Creek found their wives through the *Groom's Gazette*, Chance is not ready to make room in his life for a wife of his own. Then a letter arrives from Edmond Montgomery, a shipping agent and business associate in Wilmington, describing the dire straits of the Montgomery shipping business, his home, and family. Against his better judgment, Chance agrees to marry the man's daughter and keep what is left of the shipping finances safe for her.

What could be worse than living his life on his ranch alone? Committing to a woman who believes he is after her money.

Charity by Sylvia McDaniel

Julia by Lily Graison

Ruby by Hildie McQueen

Sarah by Peggy McKenzie

Anna by Everly West

Caroline by Lily Graison

Melody by Caroline Clemmons

Emma by Peggy McKenzie

Viola by Cyndi Raye

Ginger by Sylvia McDaniel

Abigail by Peggy McKenzie

Pearl by Hildie McQueen

Rebecca by Lily Graison

Charlotte by Kari Trumbo

Minnie by Sylvia McDaniel

Adele by Cynthia Woolf

Victoria by Maxine Douglas

Meg by Caroline Clemmons

Also by Maxine Douglas

Widows of Blessings Valley Series
Elizabeth
Vera
Stella (2025/2026)

Men of the Double K Series
Red River Crossing
Winds of Change
Game of Chance (2025)

Brides Along the Chisholm Trail Series
The Reluctant Bride
The Marshal's Bride
The Cattleman's Bride

Nashville Duets Series
Nashville Rising Star
Nashville by Morning

American Historical / Gilded Age Romance
Broken Promises (Christmas 2024)
Hannah's Discovery (Reclusive Man Series)
Leanna's Light (Book 12, Alphabet Mail-Order Brides)
Victoria (Book 19, Angel Creek Christmas Brides)
Blood Ties

Contemporary Romance / Romantic Suspense
Simply to Die For (2025)
The Gingerbread Inn (Christmas at the Inn Series)
Rings of Paradise
Knight to Remember

YA Cozy Mystery
Reading, Writing and Catmetic (Holiday Pet Sleuth Mysteries)

ACKNOWLEDGEMENT

Thank you to the authors who started the Angel Creek Christmas Brides series for asking me to take part in this year's installment.

Thank you to Maria for her patience in the time crunch. I truly appreciate all that you do

DEDICATION

To the ladies who dared to travel west and find love
in Angel Creek, Montana.

.

PROLOGUE

Wilmington, NC
Fall 1870

*L*ooking out over the port where her father's ships were once docked, the tide rose and ebbed along with Victoria Montgomery's emotions. Swiping away a tear, she turned back to the desk where her father last sat before taking his own life.

"Damn Yankee carpetbaggers! Wasn't enough they took everything that had meaning to my family, now they've taken the only thing Papa left me—his shipping business." She would not allow the Republic Bank to take what was left of her dignity.

They'd already tried to do that when she met with the bank's president, Mr. Brooks. All she'd asked for was ninety days to bring the accounts up to date. Three short months.

Still reeling from her father's death, she'd set out to take back what was rightfully hers. After going through her father's business ledgers, Victoria knew she could make up what he owed in a short amount of time. The men who had worked for her father respected and trusted her.

She'd grown up on the docks around most of them. With her father's blessing, those rough looking sailors and dockhands had been like big brothers and mentors.

In the end, it was the fact she was a woman that had let her down. Mr. Brooks told her she needed to find a husband and become a proper lady. The business was better left to a man, not a young lady grieving the loss of her father.

She'd left the bank, head held high with not a tear in sight. Inside, she was screaming out in pain. She'd let her father's loyal men down. She'd let her father down.

She'd let herself down.

But none of that mattered now. Soon she would be on a train that would begin her trip to a new life in a small mountain town in Montana Territory. And to a man her father had made her promise to agree to marry.

The match had been arranged by Father after her mother's death and before Victoria had been able to protest the ridiculous idea. She did not care there were eligible men in the West who would marry a twenty-five-year-old spinster. She loved her life and had planned on stepping in for her father when he retired.

There was nothing left for her here in Wilmington any longer. With no place to live and no prospects to speak of, she had only tales of the sea the sailors had shared with her. She loved those stories as much as she loved the sea. Now, she had only her memories to guide her on troubled waters in a landlocked town.

At least until she found a way to reclaim what was rightfully hers.

CHAPTER 1

November 1870
Ten Miles from Angel Creek, Montana

Snow began to cover the ground. A cold breeze seeped in around the leather-curtained windows. Victoria Montgomery shivered, wondering how she was expected to survive in this wilderness. She missed the wide-open salty sea air and was fast growing to resent the closed-in feeling the surrounding mountains gave her.

She longed for this journey to end yet did not look forward to the start of her new life as a wife. She knew what it took to keep a house in running order. She just never planned on being someone's wife in any way, shape, or form.

She wanted things to go back to how they were before influenza took her mother and the Republic

Bank took her father's shipping business and then, ultimately, his life. The girl she'd once been wanted to run and play on the docks. To sit on her father's lap as he read to her each night. To lick the bowl after her mother put the cake batter in the oven.

That life was gone, and nothing would ever be the same again. She would never be the same again.

The train ride had not taken nearly as long as the steamboat up the Missouri River had. For weeks, she had traveled with one stranger after another, preferring to keep to herself rather than engaging in conversation. She had nothing in common with the silly women who looked down on her plain clothes. She dressed for practicality, not fashion or looks.

Once in St. Louis, she had been able to travel by boat and say her final goodbye to the water before climbing aboard the stagecoach. Now, she sat alone in a rocking coach with no one for company but the driver, his conductor, and the occasional call from a bird of prey.

It gave her time to think. This entire journey had given Victoria time to think—too much, in fact.

She tried to imagine what the man at the end of the trail looked like. With a name like Chauncy, her imagination pictured an old miner in need of someone to cook and clean for him. Surely her father would not saddle her with that kind of a man for the rest of her days, would he?

She shivered, not from the cold but from the scraggly man her mind conjured up. Stringy gray hair that looked like it had not been washed in weeks. Cold beady eyes. Pox-marked face. Ragged, torn clothes stained with dirt and sweat.

If he wanted more than a housekeeper, Chauncy Turner had another thing coming. She would make his life so miserable that he'd send her back on the first stagecoach to North Carolina. She could not wait to put a plan in motion and return to North Carolina where she belonged as soon as she could.

Penniless or not, she didn't belong in this cold and dreary place. She belonged where the world went as far as the eye could see. She belonged home in Wilmington with the taste of the sea on her tongue. The freshness of the sea air that blew in on the wind. Not here where she sat frozen to the bone, even under a big heavy blanket.

The stage lurched to a stop, forcing Victoria to grab onto the window casing to keep in her seat. Outside, she heard the driver and his second cussing up a storm.

"Tarnation, Clyde! You drove us right into a pit and the darn wheel has broken!"

"How am I supposed to see every rut and hole under all the snow, Chester?" Clyde yelled back as he passed by the window. "Just keep the horses calm. I'll head into town and get some help as soon as everything is secure."

Victoria opened the door and was about to step out when it was all but slammed in her face.

"Stay inside, miss. It's getting darn cold out here, and the snow is comin'," Clyde cautioned her. "I'm walking into town to get help. You'd best stay under the blankets. Chester will be in after he gets the team calmed down. No sense in finding two bodies froze to death when I return."

Froze to death? Surely that was a scare tactic to keep her in her place. No one really *froze* to death, did they?

"Shouldn't we all go together?" Victoria asked, pulling her coat collar around her neck.

"No, miss." Clyde's expression softened slightly under the beard that covered his face. "It'll take a couple of hours for me to get into Angel Creek. And no disrespect, but you ain't exactly dressed for being out in this here kind of weather."

Victoria looked down at her travel clothes. Why hadn't she worn more sensible attire? The boots she wore on the docks rather than the prissy ones Mother insisted she wore as a young girl. And britches would have been more sensible as well. When she dressed in trousers and one of her father's shirts for a day at the shipping company, no one gave her a second look.

"I see what you mean," she conceded. "Tell Chester to come inside when he gets cold. I'm not so delicate as to allow a man to freeze to death."

"Yes, miss." Clyde smiled then closed her up inside the coach.

The wind began to howl, and she heard bits and pieces of the men's conversation. From what she could hear, they were arguing about Clyde walking the ten miles to Angel Creek. Chester insisting that Clyde take one of the horses since they would not be going anywhere until help arrived. After several minutes, the coach door opened and Chester bounded in, the snow swirling around him.

"Don't worry, miss. We'll have you in town in

no time at all," he assured then hunkered down into the corner of the seat across from Victoria.

She nodded and wondered if she would be getting to Angel Creek on her own two feet or carried in flat on her back.

WHILE MANY OF the men in Angel Creek had found mail-order brides, Chance Turner remained unmarried. He had given up all hope of receiving an answer to his advertisement he had posted in the *Groom's Gazette* almost a year ago. Until, that is, a few months ago when a letter arrived from Edmond Montgomery, the owner of a shipping business he had been well acquainted with in Wilmington, North Carolina. In the letter, Edmond all but pleaded with Chance to accept his daughter as his bride, citing conditions in Wilmington could ultimately leave the Montgomery girl homeless.

Before the war, Montgomery Shipping had been the only company with a ship docked in Liverpool able to accommodate Chance's needs. That of shipping a five-year-old Thoroughbred stallion with *True Briton* bloodlines from England to America.

Chance had taken up temporary residency in Wilmington along the docks waiting for his cargo to arrive. He had taken a chance on an unseen horse to begin his horse ranch in the West. He had heard stories of the vast mustang herds, and with the help of his ranch hands, they'd capture and gentle a few choice mares. He believed in his heart if he could breed a few mustang mares to Blue the foals would be the best horses for the wilderness of the West.

During those long six weeks as he waited for his future to arrive, Chance noticed the young Victoria Montgomery. She would arrive at the family business looking like a proper young lady only to appear on the docks, walking alongside her father, resembling a longshoreman.

Then the war broke out, and Blue lived up to his bloodline reputation. He was brave and strong. His surefootedness and speed saved Chance's behind more than once during the war years. And now, five years after the end of the war, Blue grazed and bred the mustang mares at Mountainridge, Chance's ranch at the base of the foothills just five miles outside of Angel Creek.

That horse and Edmond Montgomery saved his life. Chance owed it to Edmond to save his daughter's life in return. Reflecting on those six weeks, he knew back then Victoria Montgomery would make the right man a fine partner and wife. He just never expected that one day he would be the one to wed her.

He had accepted the terms which Edmond had laid out in his letter. Chance would marry Victoria, invest what was left of her fortune which now sat in the Angel Creek bank, and give her a life away from the sea. Chance did not think he'd be able to give her his heart, but he'd give her a good life and make her as happy as he could.

And that is where he was right this moment, pacing the boardwalk in front of the stagecoach office, waiting for the arrival of one Victoria Montgomery on a stage that was already several minutes late.

"Nervous are we, Chance?" Sheriff Quinn Cassidy asked, coming up behind him.

"Quinn, you have to give a guy a warning before sneaking up on him," Chance declared. "And to answer your question, only because the stage isn't here yet."

Quinn Cassidy was one of a handful of others who had come to Angel Creek to escape the aftermath of the War Between the States. He had been lucky in finding Sarah and her daughter back then. As well as the little surprise that came several months later.

Chance envied those men and their happy lives. Which was why he had finally put an advertisement in the *Gazette*. Now his dream was partially coming true—he would not be alone for the rest of his life.

"I remember how nervous I was waitin' on Sarah," Quinn chuckled. "'Course I had plenty of company that day in the church. Hard to believe it's been five years and a baby later."

"The stage is late, and now that the snow has picked up, I'm worried there's trouble on the road." Chance ignored the happy sentiment and shoved his gloved hands into the pockets of his heavy sheepskin coat.

"If it's not here soon, I'll ride out and look," Quinn offered, pulling his coat collar up around the back of his neck. "I'll swing back around after I've made my rounds."

"Thanks, Quinn," Chance said, his gaze firmly on the road that led into Angel Creek. He then walked around the wagon, checking and rechecking the harnesses and wheels. If the snow continued to fall at this rate, they would be lucky to be able to leave right after the ceremony. If not, he had better put Victoria up at Rose Haven for the night.

The sound of a rider drew his attention to the road again. The stagecoach driver, Clyde, was snow covered and hanging on to the horse's neck for dear life.

"Sheriff!" Chance called as the horse slowed enough for him to grab the loose reins. His heart sank as he pulled Clyde off the big chestnut. "Where's the stage, Clyde."

"About ten miles out. Broken wheel," was all Clyde managed to say before slipping unconscious to the ground.

Sheriff Cassidy ran up beside Chance, and together, they carried Clyde into the boardinghouse. Martha Gable already held the door open, directing them to put Clyde in one of the chairs near the parlor fireplace.

"I'll send for Dr. Walker right away," she said, pulling blankets over the nearly frozen driver. "And put some coffee and soup on. I have a feeling it'll be needed."

"Quinn, my wagon is ready. I'm going after Chester and Miss Montgomery," Chance said, not waiting for Quinn to respond. "You can stay with Clyde if you want."

"I'll be right behind you!" Quinn acknowledged, jogging toward the Sheriff's Office where his horse stood.

Chance bounded onto the toe box, snatched the reins, and gave them a swift jerk. "Walk on!" he called out, snapping the reins several more times, encouraging his team to pick up their speed.

He had to get to both Chester and Victoria; there was no time to lose.

THE COLD WIND howled, and snow continued to swirl in around the window coverings. Victoria pulled her coat closer around her and sunk deeper into a corner of the seat. She was so tired and wanted to close her eyes just for a moment.

She faintly heard Chester outside soothing the horse. From time to time, the coach rocked slightly. She was not sure if it was from the wind or if Chester was climbing up and down.

No matter which, the gentle rocking was lulling her to sleep.

Is this what "froze to death" feels like? she wondered, letting her eyelids drift shut. Visions of Wilmington and the harbor came into focus. She was home. Home to the sea. Home where she had always felt safe. She only had to open the door to her family's shipping business, and all would be right again.

The door flew open. A cold blast stung her face, and her eyes snapped open.

"Miss Montgomery?"

Victoria blinked. Did a person who was freezing to death see apparitions? If so, she loved the one looking at her.

The coach swayed slightly.

"Give me that blanket, Quinn. I think she may be in shock."

Strong arms circled her, and a man's face slowly came into focus. Beautiful emerald green eyes looked deep into hers. The warmth of a heavy blanket wrapped around her. If she was going to die, at least it would be in the arms of this man, whoever he was.

"We've got to get her to town. Help me get her into the wagon, Chester." The man who held her in his arms ordered.

Her body rose then shifted back and forth until she lay on a flat surface. The snow continued to swirl around her, pulling her into a kaleidoscope. The cold did its best to cut through the warmth enveloping her.

"Ride in the back with her and talk to her as much as you can, Chester" a third distant voice ordered as another blanket covered her. "I'll ride ahead and let Dr. Walker know he's got another patient, Chance."

"We'll be right behind you, Sheriff."

The wagon lurched forward, and the world faded away.

CHAPTER 2

"How's she doing, Chester?" Chance called out, glancing over his shoulder through the falling snow.

"She's passed out but breathing."

The words, almost lost amongst the swirling snow in the cold wind, were enough for Chance to throw caution to the wind. His gut wrenched into a painful knot. He had no choice; time was of the essence. He had to get his bride to town, and there was no time to lose.

"Yaw!" he yelled, snapping the reins, encouraging the team of horses to move quicker through the snow and wind. The ten miles of trail lost under a blanket of white, he kept pushing the team forward until the grey outline of the town buildings came into view.

The wagon thundered into Angel Creek, causing people to scatter. Chance pulled up in front of Rose Haven where Doctor Nicholas Walker stood waiting. Before Chance's feet hit the ground, Nick was at the side of the wagon.

"Quickly, get her inside!" Nick ordered, hurrying up the porch steps in front of Chance.

Chance held Victoria tight against his chest after Chester lowered her into his arms, her scent enveloping him. She smelled like the sea—salty and fresh. A soft moan escaped, giving him hope they had arrived in time.

"You're safe now," he whispered in her ear as he walked through the open door.

"On the chaise lounge in the parlor," Martha instructed, closing the door behind them.

Setting her down as if she were a fragile china doll, Chance moved a stray strand of hair from across her pale face.

The woman he now gazed at bore no resemblance to the vivacious girl he'd seen years ago. The light of life was no longer present on her face. Her cheeks did not carry the blush of sweet innocence. She looked sullen and pale.

He feared he may have lost her.

"I will need to examine her, Chance," Nick said over his shoulder with the authority of a medical expert.

Chance nodded, then reluctantly stepped back as Nick dug into his medical bag.

"How long has she been unconscious?" Nick asked while checking Victoria's vitals.

"Moments after we placed her in the wagon, I think," Chance answered, looking over Nick's shoulder. His heart pounded as fear overtook his senses. How could he be so sure when he had not been the one next to her in the back of the wagon?

What if Chester lied to him? No, he would not give in to the what-ifs when there was no proof to them. Victoria would live if he had anything to do with it. And right now, he felt as helpless as a newborn colt finding its legs.

"She has to be alright," he said, clutching his hands as tightly as the muscles compressing around his heart. The force of emotion caught him off guard. Was it because if she died his promise to protect her would have failed? Or was it something else? Something only his heart knew. Something he was yet to discover.

"Martha, would you please help in getting her out of this wet coat? Then she will need a warm quilt and some hot soup for when she wakes," Nick said, looking over his shoulder at Rose Haven's kindly owner.

Martha nodded and helped remove Victoria's outerwear, then scurried out of the room in search of what Nick requested.

"She'll be fine, Chance. She's a strong woman," Nick assured, standing over his patient. "Is this your bride?"

Yes." Chance knelt beside Victoria, taking her hand in his. "Victoria Montgomery. She's the daughter of a shipping magnate out of Wilmington who I'd done some business with."

"I can see you are worried, but don't fear. She'll wake up soon enough, and Martha will make sure she has some hot soup." Nick patted his shoulder then turned away as Martha covered Victoria with the requested quilts. "You'll be married as planned, just not as soon as you first thought."

"I certainly do hope so, Nick," he said searching for any sign of his once not wanted bride to stir. Now, more than his promise to Edmond, Chance wanted to protect Victoria for the rest of his days.

But would he ever be able to love her?

THE SALTY BREEZE and lapping waves settled calmly over her. The sea had always been her true friend in times of trouble. Papa always said the sea air cleared his mind. And it always did hers as well.

Except now the whispers in the distance would not go away. They surrounded her like fingers of the wind constantly tugging at her. Pushing and pulling her toward them. Back toward the shore where the whispers grew closer and she struggled to see their origin through the fog.

Why can't I open my eyes? I hear voices around me. Who is here? Mama? Papa?

Panic filtered through Victoria's mind. Was she dead? If so, why hadn't her parents come to greet her at the Gates of Heaven?

The icy fingers of darkness gave way to a soothing warmth, but only slightly.

"Martha, do you have any soup ready?" a male voice barked, very much in control.

"Yes, Doctor. Shall I get some?" A woman's worried yet comforting voice answered.

Doctor? Am I in an infirmary?

"Yes, I have a feeling Miss Montgomery may join us soon."

At least the doctor sounds encouraging. How does this person know me?

Footsteps echoed in the darkness then faded away.

"Are you sure, Nick?"

Nick? Searching the darkness of her mind, Victoria found no reference to anyone she knew by the name of Nick.

"Yes, her vitals have been growing stronger. And the color has begun to return to her face." The doctor reassured the new voice she heard in the distance sounded vaguely familiar.

"Will Victoria be all right?" Concern and compassion edged his words, his voice soft yet all male. Gooseflesh crept over her body. Where had she heard it before?

"Your bride may be tired for a few days but will fully recover. No need to worry about that."

Bride? Did I marry someone? I must have for they speak as if they know me well. But I don't recognize their voices. No, I didn't get married! I'm sure of it.

What is that wonderful aroma? Is someone cooking? I must wake up! Please Lord, allow me to see the light again.

"Martha, the soup smells wonderful."

"I have brought enough for both of you. Clyde and Chester are in the kitchen, filling their bellies as well," Martha replied, pride in her voice. Obviously, a woman who enjoyed taking care of people—even strangers. This might be someone she would like to get to know—if she ever woke up, that was.

"Chance, have some soup."

Chance? Why does that name sound familiar?

"No, Nick. I will not eat until Victoria wakes," the voice called Chance replied quietly.

I'm so thirsty. Victoria licked her parched lips. She tried to move her arms, her fingers but couldn't. *What has ahold of my hand? Who are these people? Why can't I move my fingers?*

Her fingers twitched within the warmth surrounding them. The darkness subsided. First grey then light.

Opening her eyes, she stared at the figure sitting next to her. It was so close she could feel the warmth that was the vision from the stagecoach.

"Am I dead?"

THE RELIEF FLOODING Chance was unlike anything he had felt before. Yes, he had a similar feeling before. Once, when the Montgomery ship from England began to dock and his stud finally arrived safely. Also, when the bloodshed from the war had finally come to an end, and he returned home to find his family all but gone from the years of turmoil.

But this. This felt as if his life had been given back to him. Just when had he lost it?

Holding her hand in his, afraid to let go for fear she would slip away back into the darkness, he gently caressed it with the pad of his thumb. "You are very much alive, Victoria."

"You gave us quite a fright, my dear," Martha said from the end of the chaise lounge.

"As soon as Doc Walker says you can travel,

we'll get you proper clothing for this country. The winters here can be frigid and are nowhere near as mild as Wilmington's. Then we will see about the preacher marrying us, and we can go home.

"But first, I think you should have a little something to eat." Chance picked up a bowl of soup from the tray Martha had set on the table beside the chaise. "Martha's potato soup is the best you can find."

Victoria sat straighter, her gaze studying him closely. Too closely. Did she recognize him? She had been a mere young lady when last he saw her, flitting in and out of her father's office. He was five years her senior and now had a beard that hid the face she might remember.

"Why should I marry you when I've already been saddled to another man?" Her eyes sparked as she reached for the bowl.

"Yes, I know you are." Chance grew nervous as her piercing brown eyes bored into him. Would she reject him and their marriage agreement?

"I'm sorry there wasn't time to be properly introduced. Getting you into town and seen by the doctor was foremost on my mind. I felt you were in urgent need of medical attention before…" He did not want to imagine what losing her might have meant. A promise to protect her broken, for one. Chance shook what could have been from his mind. He did not want those cobwebs clouding his senses. "My name is Chauncy Turner, but everyone calls me Chance. I am the man you've agreed to marry, Miss Montgomery."

"You mean the man *my father* agreed for me to

marry, don't you?" Victoria corrected with venom in her words. Her eyes sparked with a challenge to deny the truth.

He could not deny what she said. He was the man her father, not Victoria, had arranged to marry his daughter. Edmond only wanted to protect his daughter and what was left of their fortune. But she didn't know that, did she?

There it was. The one element that could get both of them out of this marriage agreement. He could give her the opportunity to refuse to marry him. She had every right to break an agreement she had nothing to do with making. Except, Chance had made a promise to Edmond Montgomery to look after his daughter. And then there was the matter of Victoria's money safely tucked away in the bank. He would not go back on his agreement whether Victoria wanted it or not.

"Yes, your father made the marriage arrangements. I'm sorry for your loss. Your father was a great man," Chance said softly, feeling the shipping business had lost a great and honest man. "Are you considering not honoring them?"

Chance held his breath. He could not make her marry him. And he certainly would not make her since she'd not been the one to agree to their union. Hell, who was he trying to convince? The moment he held her in his arms, he knew he wanted her.

If she did want to break the marriage agreement, what about her money in the bank waiting for her? He had put it in her name as a separate account from the ranch. Chance had done as her father asked him to do. So, he did what he had to do to safeguard Victoria's money—or what was left of it after the carpetbaggers tried to take it all. Luckily, Edmond had seen the writing on the wall and acted accordingly before it had happened.

"Well, Miss Montgomery?" He released her hand and sat back in the chair, studying her face. "Will you abide by your father's agreement and do the honorable thing of becoming my wife? Or not?"

The room suddenly became still and heavy as he waited for Victoria's answer.

CHAPTER 3

ictoria studied the man who was to be her husband. She could do worse in the scheme of things. This man, Chauncy Turner, seemed kind, and he was not bad to look at. But would he love her? Or would he resent her for taking his freedom?

Would she resent him for taking hers? She knew she could never love a man she had not chosen.

Papa chose him for a reason. He must have trusted this man enough to put me in his care. How can I go back on Papa's word? I can't, without feeling shame for letting him down. A promise is a promise, and I've never broken one before.

I don't have to let Mr. Turner know that, do I?

"You are right, this is really good soup," she commented, not wanting to broach the subject of her upcoming marital status until she had some sort of plan. "Would you share the recipe with me some time, Mrs.—I'm sorry, I don't know your name."

"No need for formality in Angel Creek, my dear. Everyone calls me Martha." Martha beamed with pride. Victoria's heart warmed, knowing how a simple compliment could mean so much to a person. "Of course, I will. You can consider it a wedding gift."

"Wedding?" Victoria spurted, wiping her mouth with the napkin offered by the man she was to wed. Maybe she should use it to wipe the crooked grin off his face instead. She did not see anything funny in spitting out perfectly good soup like some street urchin.

"Goodness, have I said something wrong?" Martha asked, her kind eyes sparkling with concern. "You came all this way to marry Chance, didn't you?"

"Victoria, Miss Montgomery, hasn't—"

"What Mr. Turner is trying to say is that I haven't had time to consider the idea of marriage," Victoria interjected, not only to save her own hide but Chauncy's as well. She should have let him stumble on, but she did not have the heart since he drove through the snowstorm to save her life.

Her debt was now paid to him, as far as she was concerned. Yet she might never be rid of him if she honored her father's desire for her to marry this man.

Why would her father choose this man, or any man for that matter, for her to marry? Did he have something on her family that he threatened to use? A debt that needed to be settled, and this was how it was to be wiped clean?

Why else would her father take away her freedom to become an independent woman?

"Miss Montgomery, it was a pleasure to meet you although the circumstances could have been better," Doctor Walker said while packing his medical bag. "I'm sure my wife Melody will be excited to know another southern lady has arrived in Angel Creek."

"Thank you, Doctor." Victoria smiled, relieved to know there was another woman in town who would surely be sympathetic to her situation. But would it be wise for her to grow an alliance so soon? "I look forward to meeting your wife one day soon."

"Give her a day or two, Chance, before you take her out to that ranch of yours. Good day, everyone." Doctor Walker tilted his hat and chuckled as he walked out the door.

"I'll leave you two to work things out. If you need me, I'll be in the kitchen," Martha said as she gathered up the soiled dishes.

"Did I miss something?" Victoria asked, looking from the amused look on Martha's face to the guarded one on Chauncy's. "You own a— ranch?"

"WHY? DO YOU have an objection to that?" Chance asked as her expression went from surprise to anger. What could possibly make her angry about him being a rancher? His family had been ranching for generations. "It's honest work, and I make a good living at it."

"Should I?" Victoria all but spat at him. Then her face softened, and she looked at him through lowered lashes. "I am sorry. Nothing about this entire situation surprises me. I thought you lived in town, near civilization in this godforsaken country. Not out God-knows-where without a store or doctor or people nearby. Isn't it enough I had to give up my life by the sea to come here? What was my father thinking?"

"Probably wanted someone he trusted to take care of you," Chance muttered pushing out of the chair. "I know your father wanted only what is best for you. That's why he asked me to look after you before he …."

"I don't need anyone to take care of me! And if you knew my father at all, which you obviously didn't, you'd know he would never ask a man, any man, to take care of me. My parents taught me how to take care of myself."

"Maybe 'take care of' wasn't the correct term or one that you wanted to hear. Understand your father was looking out for your best interests. Nothing is certain after that damn war, as you well know."

Stuffing his hands into his pockets to keep from strangling her, Chance crossed over to the picture window. The snow had let up, and the sun twinkled off the blanket of white. With any luck, they should be able to get on their way in the next day or two. That may give him enough time to squelch any idea of backing out of this madness. He also might have enough time to figure out how to tell Victoria she wasn't as destitute as she thought.

"I did know your father, probably better than most." Chance started to regret the course of this conversation. He'd had no intention of confessing anything to her until they'd had time to settle into their life together. Unless their marriage was consummated before Christmas. "I'm not surprised you don't remember me; you were quite the strong-headed young lady trying to be a dockhand.

"Tomorrow, we can go over to the mercantile and get you a good pair of boots and a warm coat as well." Chance turned away from the window to find Victoria only a few feet from him. His body responded to the lofty scent of her nearness. He'd have to be more aware of her in the future. The last person to sneak up on him was dead.

In two steps, he was by her side, his heart still pounding in his chest. "Shouldn't you be laying down?"

"Out of all the men my father did busines with, why would he choose you, a Yankee? The very people who destroyed his life. The very people who caused him to lose his business. The very people who pushed him into taking his own life. The very people who took everything and everyone that mattered to me."

Her accusing gaze fixed on him. If he was running from something, there was no place for him to hide under that pointed look. Luckily, he wasn't running any more than he had been before the war.

A tear slipped down her cheek. He stopped short of taking her in his arms and kissing away the anger that marred her heart. As much as he hated seeing a woman cry, Victoria needed to feel her pain freely before she would begin to heal and live again.

He'd thought the long arm of the war wouldn't reach him in the mountains, yet here it was staring him in the face. Guilty by association.

His life here was peaceful and uncomplicated—just the way he liked it. But that was all about to change; he could feel it in his bones.

HER HEART STUTTERED in her chest; warm shivers caressed her as she watched him watching her.

There must be something her father trusted about him. What it might be, Victoria couldn't imagine. She didn't know anything about this man except for one thing.

Chauncy Turner was a Yankee, after all! A Yankee with beautiful eyes and thick, dark hair neatly settled above his cotton shirt collar. And that crooked smile of his could melt the snow outside.

Maybe I'm being a bit harsh on him, Victoria thought, second-guessing her conflicting emotions. *He should never had agreed to Papa's request in the first place. Papa should have told me of his intentions, before… I will not fall under his spell.*

"I'm not sure what my father had in mind. He didn't live long enough to tell me his plan. He only made me promise to honor the marriage contract," she said with false bravado, swallowing the grief building inside. "So, I made a promise to abide by his arrangement with you before he took his own life. I'll not go back on Papa's word or I wouldn't have left North Carolina."

Her body trembled suddenly. Blackness threatened to take her once again. Tears rolled down her cheeks, and she found herself wrapped in the tenderness of Chance's arms

"If it helps, I'm not sure what he intended either. All I know is he asked me to protect you by marrying you. Maybe I should have questioned his motives, but I didn't," Chance whispered against her ear.

His breath felt like feathers upon her hair and skin. His tenderness a surprising welcome she didn't want. His magic wove around her like a gentle, comforting breeze. The blackness disappeared, clarity taking its place.

Victoria liked his arms around her. She very much liked it, in fact. She felt that sense of security and safety that had been taken from her life.

Pushing out of his arms, she turned away from unwanted feelings. She didn't want to like this man. Furthermore, she didn't want anything to do with him.

"I'm sorry. I'm not one who is generally given to having spells." Feeling betrayed by her own body's desire for wanting to be in his arms again, Victoria put some distance between them.

"Mr. Turner, it seems to me that we both have made a promise neither of us really wants to keep." Victoria collected herself and held her head high, keeping her resolve. "Is that true?"

The conflicting emotions in his eyes puzzled her. Certainly, he couldn't seriously be considering going on with the sham of a marriage. She was giving him a way out if he wanted it. It wasn't too late for her to go back to Wilmington. Or for him to go back to his ranch—alone.

"Victoria, may I call you that?" Chance asked, taking a step closer, causing her to back away. "After all, if we are to be married, it would be less cause for gossip, don't you agree?"

Well, that's that. He plans on going through with this marriage after all. I have no choice—again.

"Yes, you may," Victoria conceded. "And I shall call you Chauncey?"

"Chance. My friends call me Chance," he said, a twinkle in his eye and that smile of his working magic on her weakening resolve. "Including your father."

"A friend who never graced our doorstep, I might add," Victoria pointed out.

"True enough, but a friend none the less." Chance nodded in agreement. "Be that as it may, you didn't answer my question. Will you marry me as agreed by your father or not?"

Nibbling her bottom lip, Victoria contemplated what to do next. Would he agree to modifying her father's initial arrangements?

"With some conditions," she quickly said, her mind racing for a solution. Any solution to be rid of the man.

"Such as?"

"I want my own room." She paced the room, getting as far from him as possible. His nearness unnerved her, and she didn't like the way her body responded. "And if we are to take meals together, they should not be of the romantic type. They shall be as if I were a boarder in your house."

"Simple enough. The sleeping arrangements have already been made. Our rooms are on different floors." Chance smiled, stuffing his hands into his pockets. "As for taking meals together, there may be many days that you will be doing so alone. My ranch sometimes demands long hours away."

"Since I have come to you penniless, you will also provide for me whatever I may need or want," she informed, hoping her lack of finances would sway him to decline and give up this ridiculous farce.

"I believe I have already given that indication, but yes, I am prepared to give you what you need—or want." Chance took a step closer then stopped. The smile on his face matched the one in his eyes. Damn but he was a charmer!

"Then we are in agreement that this is a temporary arrangement?" Had she won a victory of sorts? "In addition, you must agree if we find we aren't a match by Christmas, the marriage will be dissolved."

"Yes, I am in agreement." Chance extended a hand. "Unless our marriage is consummated as is customary for mail-order brides arriving in Angel Creek, then I'm afraid we will be man and wife for life."

Well, there it is! My way out of this marriage not of my choosing. No way am I gracing his bed.

"Then I shall become your wife, in name only, until Christmas," Victoria agreed, shaking her soon-to-be husband's hand, appalled at the way her stomach fluttered.

CHAPTER 4

Two days later

Chance glanced over at his wife.

His wife! A term he thought he'd never have use for. Admittedly, the more the idea of Victoria being his wife echoed in his head for the past few days, the more he'd gotten used to it. Unfortunately, she was his in name only. He would never truly have the right to be her husband. He was sure she'd see to that between now and Christmas.

Chance was bound to keep his agreement with both Victoria and her father. The one time he damned himself for being a man of honor. But he was, and so he'd keep his wife safe until at least Christmas. After that, she'd be on her own.

"Are you warm enough? It is going to take a good while before we arrive at the ranch," Chance said, holding back the urge to reach over and tuck the wool blanket firmly around her lap. She was shivering like a leaf.

"Yes, but you need not worry. I am used to taking care of myself well enough," Victoria informed him with her gaze straight ahead and her tone matter-of-fact.

He understood her fear and her anger. She'd not been given any time to consider her own fate; it had been decided for her. Victoria was a woman who'd lost control of her life, and it must not be sitting well with her. Mix that in with losing the life she'd expected to live, and it wasn't any wonder she was out of sorts.

During their marriage ceremony, she'd barely glanced at him as Reverend Carroll performed the service. The vows she'd repeated mere whispers on the wind. As if the words of promise were no more than a second thought. He knew they were said out of a sense of duty. If he failed to make her feel at ease with their situation, life would be unbearable between them between now and Christmas.

"I must apologize for the way our union was not as you may have imagined or wanted it to be." Chance glanced sideways at her. He was used to travelling the road home in silence, but he was usually alone. Having a companion made he feel he needed to conduct polite conversation.

Or at least try since his travel companion was his wife.

"You'll come to love Angel Creek in time," he assured, failing miserably if the stiffness in her back was any indication of her reaction.

"I don't foresee that sentiment happening since our marriage is on paper only, unless we—well you know," Victoria chirped, sitting very still. Her gaze, trained on the road ahead, didn't flinch once. He knew from experience if she didn't relax, she'd feel the cold more. Besides, he wasn't much looking forward to carrying a nearly frozen woman into the house—again. Why did he have the feeling it was going to be a long ride back to the ranch?

"May I make a suggestion, Victoria?"

"And what might that be?" She glanced over at him, suspicion darkening her beautiful brown eyes. "That with time I will forget all that was dear to me in Wilmington, I suppose? That with time—"

"No, not at all. It is only if you could relax a bit more and notice the beauty around you, you may not feel the cold as much. I can see you shivering, even with the blanket."

He grinned as she took a deep breath and her body automatically relaxed. Under normal circumstances, he may have properly courted Victoria at one time. But the war and its aftermath didn't permit life to be normal as they once knew it before the fighting began.

Chance wasn't going to let that stop him from admiring his beautiful wife who'd once been a very willful young lady. Had she outgrown that youthful rebellious stage or had her father continued to encourage it, not having a son to carry on with the business?

In the end, it didn't matter. He was the only one who knew all Victoria had left of her life in Wilmington was the money she knew nothing about. And he couldn't let her find out until their agreement had been fulfilled on or before

Christmas.

AS MUCH AS she didn't want to admit it, Victoria noticed the splendor of the mountains and foothills, and the way the snow glistened off them like tiny diamonds. She'd also never admit that her husband's suggestion to relax had indeed subsided her shivering in the cold.

Husband!

Victoria barely remembered the ceremony or the lovely winter bouquet Martha had assembled for her. She had recited the words, or had she? Of course, she had, or she wouldn't be on this wagon with the feel of a ring on her left hand.

The only thing that stuck out in her mind was the preacher reminding them their union was indeed on paper only. Unless they consummated it before Christmas that is. Was luck finally on her side and given her a way to be independent again?

She glanced over at Chance, the man she was now married to but hadn't chosen for herself. A handsome sort of man who caused her tummy to flutter when he so much as glanced her way.

Victoria was sure she wouldn't have trouble keeping her resolve true between now and Christmas. Living with Chance would definitely put her to task, and she wasn't about to give more than she bargained for to him. The had until the holiday to see if their union worked. If not, then she would demand he pay for her fare on the first stage back to Wilmington.

"You said you had done some business with my father?" she asked, needing to know if there was a weakness she could use to her advantage to get out of this so-called marriage.

"Yes, before the war," Chance said in a low timbre that could shake a young woman's determination. Just not hers, if she had any say in it.

"May I ask what it was? There were so many shipments at that time, it's no wonder I don't remember you," she said, knowing full well which side he'd fought on. Not that it really mattered. She was not going to be here long enough to care one way or the other.

"I'm not surprised. You were young and more interested in the activity on the docks as I recall," he chucked warmly then gifted her with a grin that melted her resolve a little.

She did not think he was laughing at her or criticizing her. She felt it was quite the opposite. She had seen enough of those disapproving looks over the years to know one when she saw it. And there was none of that on Chance's face or in the way he grinned at her.

"Yes, well, be that as it may." She did not care if he disapproved of her desire to be on the docks or not. That was between her and her father. Or it had been. "You didn't answer my question."

"Edmond was the only shipper from the area to have a ship in England capable of bringing back my cargo." His chest puffed out like a peacock even under the heavy winter coat. "A stud horse with one of the finest English bloodlines."

"That was your horse?" she gasped. Victoria well remembered the big and beautiful black stallion. He was the most magnificent animal she had ever seen.

"You remember then?" Chance asked, sounding surprised.

"The horse, yes. The man, no." Victoria immediately realized how horrible the words sounded, even though truthful. "I'm sorry, but that stallion was magnificent."

"I didn't realize you knew anything about horses." Chance glanced at her, sending warmth through her chilled bones.

"Only enough to get into trouble, I'm afraid," she laughed. "I still know quality when I see it. Papa taught me a few things growing up."

"I'M SURE HE did, as it shows," Chance agreed, not really sure how he felt having an independent woman for a wife. "I have no doubt he was preparing you to take over the business. Or at the very least, guiding your husband.

"That may have sounded presumptuous of me, but it wasn't meant to be. It's that most women would have married by now. And—never mind. It really doesn't matter at this point, does it?"

Chance had not wanted to start their first day of marriage criticizing his new wife. Those old ways of thinking had surfaced out of nowhere. He well knew how the war had changed not only men, but women as well. Angel Creek was a prime example with so many former Southern bells living totally different lives. And happily, at that.

"It doesn't matter what you think, Chance." Victoria cast him a fleeting glance. "After all, this marriage between us will be over soon, and we can both go back to our normal lives having honored my father's dying wish."

Chance only nodded. He needed to think. Re-evaluate.

He had to think about keeping her in his life and her money tucked away in the bank safe. He had to think of a way to get Victoria to agree to stay with him.

These past few days, having to worry and fuss over Victoria, brought something out of him. He found he liked having someone to care about. Looked forward to seeing her every day while she was recuperating at the boarding house.

Maybe he had been too quick to agree the marriage terms.

Maybe Victoria was just what he needed.

Two too many maybes to worry about right now. He had to get them home to the ranch, and the herd closer to the barn before winter really set in. Then he would worry about trying to square things with his wife. Chance snapped the reins, encouraging the team to move out a little quicker.

"What happened to the stallion?" Victoria asked, shifting and brushing up against him.

"Huh?" That brief encounter was just enough to make him forget what she asked. Chance glanced down at her. The space between them, reduced to less than an inch, sparked.

"The horse you had shipped from England, what happened to him?"

"Oh, Blue is everything I thought he would be," he bragged then shook his head. "I didn't realize how that must have sounded to you. I usually don't boast about things, but that horse saved my life in more ways than one, it seems."

"So, you still have him then?" Victoria asked, surprised.

"Yes. He has produced some fine colts with the mustangs I've been lucky enough to catch," Chance answered.

"How has he saved your life? It doesn't seem possible that an animal could do such a thing," Victoria asked, sounding genuinely interested.

"I suppose not to most people." Chance pushed the horror of the war far from his mind. "Ole Blue got me out of many scrapes during the war. If not for him, I may not be here today.

"It won't be long now. We are finally on my land, and the ranch house isn't much further up the road." Chance wanted nothing more than to get home before she asked anything about the war. It was a dark time, and he didn't want to relive it again.

CHAPTER 5

Victoria sat quietly as the silence between them grew. Had everything they needed to say been said since their vows? She doubted that very much. Chance didn't strike her as the type to stay silent for long. And, as her papa pointed out many times, neither was she.

The wagon lurched forward as the horses picked up speed. They knew they were almost home. How she envied the creatures. To know when you are home again. What she wouldn't give to be within sight of Wilmington. Of her home.

And then there it was—home—and it took her breath away.

A two-story log house with a front porch suitable for summer evenings looked to be sitting at the base of a snow-covered hill. The mountain rose like a sentry keeping watch over those at its feet.

"We're home, Mrs. Turner." Chance pulled the horses and wagon to a stop in front of the porch.

"I'll get your things up to your room after I get you inside."

"I never imagined it would look so beautiful," Victoria said in awe as Chance helped her down from the wagon. His large hands gently encased her waist. Their gazes locked, and she paused for a moment before slipping out of his hold on her.

"Out here, you can see nature's beauty the buildings in town seem to mask." Chance took her elbow and led her up the porch to the front door.

Turning the knob, he pushed the door open with a foot.

"Oh!" Victoria cried out, surprised to have been swept up in his arms and immediately carried across the threshold and into her new life. As fleeting as it may be.

Still in his arms, they stood for a moment in the living room. The heady scent of musk and woods and horses wafted into her senses. She closed her eyes for a moment and let herself get lost in the smell of her husband. This would be as close to him as she'd ever allow herself to be again, and she wanted to commit it to memory before he released her. To remind herself whey she'll never have the kind of love match her heart desired. One of mutual choosing.

"I'll go get your things," Chance said, setting her down lightly. "Feel free to look over the pantry. If you feel there is something we may need, please make note of it. I try to keep it well stocked with winter approaching. It may be some time before we are able to get to town."

"So, you're saying we could be trapped out

here?" The high-pitched words hitched in her throat. How would she be able to leave if they couldn't get to town?

"Maybe for several days, but not all winter long. So, there's no need to worry." Chance chuckled as he walked out, closing the door behind him.

Victoria shivered slightly and took a turn around the front room. It was rather large and felt homey with dark braided rugs scattered on the floor. Large furniture was organized in such a way that any conversation would include anyone who visited. A sofa and two comfortable looking chairs faced each other. The stone fireplace on the wall opposite the kitchen had logs arranged in the hearth, ready to provide warmth.

The kitchen, while not as large as the one she'd had back home, was still spacious enough to work in. She was pleased to find a cast-iron stove, a pie safe, and an icebox. There was a window over the sink facing the foothills, and she imagined the view was lovely in the spring. Opening the cupboard doors one by one, she found a full set of dishes, glasses, cups, and various sizes of mixing bowls. A large tin held silverware, and another next to the bowls had cooking utensils in it.

It seemed her husband kept a tidy house and had thought of everything needed to make a meal or bake a pie or two. The pantry was indeed well stocked, and she didn't find a thing that was needed. Disappointment at not needing anything edged her heart as the front door opened, allowing a rush of cold air in.

Chance had one of her trunks in his arms as he kicked the door shut. She couldn't take her eyes off of him as he headed up the stairs to her room. A large thud on the floor, followed by footsteps on the stairs, signaled her husband was returning.

"I better get this fire going. It is a bit chilly in here, don't you think?" It only took him a few moments before the fire's red and orange glow began to fill the room with warmth.

"Have you had time to explore the pantry? Is there anything you think is needed?" he asked, stoking the fire until it blazed.

"No. You have done well in providing what you thought was needed. Everything seems to be in order." Victoria stood in front of the fireplace, unbuttoning her coat as her body was finally warm from the ride in the cold. "Where do you sleep?"

"In this room." Chance walked over to a door that stood ajar. "That room over there has a copper tub in it. Upstairs, you'll find your room and a place for all your things, as well as a smaller tub should you desire to bathe in privacy. I ordered items I thought a woman would like and need. I relied on my memory of my mother's furnishings, so I hope they are to your liking.

"I may have built this house out away from town, but that didn't mean I had to give up some luxuries I grew up with," Chance informed, heading out the door once again.

Victoria slipped out of the heavy coat they'd bought at the mercantile and hung it on the coatrack. She heard heavy footsteps outside the door and pulled it open for Chance to carry the last of her things into the house to her room.

When he returned, he paused for a moment at the bottom of the stairs, his eyes looking her over. A smile peeked at the corners of his mouth and hidden dimples appeared, making him all the more charming. "I'll be in the barn for a bit. If you'd like to start cooking a meal for us, please do," Chance said as he walked back out the door.

She watched from the window as Chance turned the horses and wagon toward the barn. Breathing deeply, she headed up the stairs to her room. She had unpacking and some thinking to do.

Then she might begin making herself at home in the kitchen.

CHANCE UNHITCHED THE team then led the horses into their respective stalls. One by one he ran a stiff brush across their backs as they munched down the hay left in the morning.

Under normal circumstances, he would have gone straight back up to the house after putting the horses up for the night. Except, this was no ordinary day. It was the day he married a woman with terms to get out of the marriage. Terms he'd agreed to.

Did he really want to stay with a woman who may not want to be with him?

Maybe. Maybe not. All he was sure of was that he'd fulfilled his obligation to Edmond Montgomery by marrying his daughter and tucking her money safely away. Once Christmas came, things would go back to normal.

He'd go back to his lonely life on the ranch.

Victoria could go back to her life in

Wilmington, whatever that might be with enough money to live in comfort.

He could have put a stop to this before it began by giving her the money and sending her back to Wilmington. Instead, he'd let his honor and her beauty cloud his judgment.

And beautiful she was. Hair the color of dark honey and eyes so richly brown they could make a blind man see again.

So just what was he doing here in the barn while Victoria got settled in his—their—home?

Closing and securing the stall doors, he tossed the brush onto a hay bale then hung the harness on a peg next to the bridles. The wagon was fine where it was. All that was left was for him to close the barn doors and head back to the cabin.

Instead, he plopped down on the nearest bale of hay.

"What in the world have I gotten myself into?" Chance asked aloud, shaking his head, running both hands over his face. "If I let Victoria have her way and she goes back home, am I going against my promise? Or doesn't it really matter since I did marry the girl and put her money safely away in the bank?

"Lord, I need guidance." He bowed his head and prayed. With a deep sigh, Chance pushed himself off the hay. "And patience."

Glancing once more around the darkening barn, Chance walked out the massive barn doors built to keep the snow, cold, and predators out, then secured them behind him.

VICTORIA HAD UNPACKED only what was necessary for a few weeks from her trunks while Chance had gone to the barn to do chores. Once everything was in its place, she'd taken a good look around her bedroom.

The featherbed had fresh linens on it, and a lovely yet subtle quilt in various shades of blues on a white background spilled over the edges. A chest of drawers butted up against the wall opposite the bed. A simple, functional vanity and chair sat near the window that overlooked the front yard and foothills. A washstand stood on the other side of heavily laced windows.

And, as Chance had indicated, a small copper tub sat in the small room just outside the bedroom door. There was also, to her surprise, a chamber pot which she suspected would be up to her to take care of.

Her husband had indeed thought of all her needs except one. She wouldn't be here long enough to warrant all his handiwork. Still, she was pleased by his efforts to make her feel comfortable.

Now it was up to her to be as pleasant as she could be. And since she was hungry, she'd at least fix them something to eat.

But what?

Victoria scrounged around the pantry until she found all she needed for a simple yet filling meal. Fried potatoes and onions with salt pork.

Gathering the food items in her arms, she placed everything on the counter and began to heat up the stove. Grabbing a cast-iron skillet, she sliced up the salt pork and placed it and a small amount of lard inside. Satisfied the heat was sufficient, she placed the skillet on the stove and turned to slice the potatoes and onions. Tossing them into a bowl, she seasoned the mixture with a bit of salt and some pepper before adding them to the salt pork.

The sizzle and aroma of the pork made her realize how hungry she was. She gave the mixture a quick turn with a wooden spoon then went back to the sink to clean up the peelings.

She glanced out the window. The snow was beginning to fall again. A sense of peacefulness fell over her. Not quite like watching the tide come in but just as serene.

Beautiful and, she bet, just as dangerous.

She knew how to survive when the wind and rain raged, but not when the cold and snow would surely come. For the several weeks she'd be here, she'd do what she could to get through until she went back home.

The sizzling on the stove reminded her that if she wasn't careful, they'd be eating burnt food for supper. Turning the items over and over, the potatoes turned a rich golden color and the pork crisped up nicely.

Moving the skillet over to another burner to keep warm but stop cooking, she pulled some plates and silverware from the cupboard. As she placed a set of the items on either end of the table, the door blew open and her tummy flipped.

Her husband had returned.

CHAPTER 6

hance smelled the richness of the salt pork, fried potatoes, and onions before he opened the door.

"Smells good, Tori," he said, not even thinking what he'd just called Victoria.

"Who's Tori?" Victoria turned from the stove, the hot skillet in her hand. "A former lover from the past?"

"No, it's you. Victoria is such a long name that I thought to use Tori when we're together." Shrugging out of his coat and boots, Chance waited while his perturbed wife served the meal and set the skillet back on the stove.

"Would have been polite if you had asked me first," she scolded, sitting down then pouring coffee into her cup, leaving him to pour his own. "However, since I may not be here long, I don't see any harm in it. Please don't use it in front of others."

"Of course not, if that is what you want." Pulling out the chair opposite Victoria, relief flooded Chance. Looking at his plate, he cut into the meat and took a small bite.

If his wife was a horrible cook, he didn't want to spit anything out onto his plate. He thought he could manage to swallow a small piece much easier than a healthy portion.

To his surprise, the meat tasted as good as it smelled. And the potatoes were fried to perfection. So, his wife could cook!

Glancing up, he watched Victoria pushing her food around the plate. She had neatly separated the potatoes from the meat. How strange, since she'd cooked everything in the same skillet. He wondered if she always ate this way.

"Did you see it's snowing again?" Chance asked, breaking the deafening silence forming between them.

"I did. Do you think it will last very long?" Victoria's question was edged with worry.

"It might. The heavy snow is a bit later than usual this year." Chance didn't want to alarm her into thinking she'd have no way out if she chose. She just wouldn't be able to leave as soon as she might think if they got snowed in. Which, as far as he was concerned, wouldn't be such a bad idea.

It would give them time to get to know each other.

"Heavy? How heavy?"

There it was. The fear on her face he'd wanted to avoid. When would he learn not to be so blunt? Now he had to smooth things over before she went running out the door.

"Tori, we are at the base of the mountains. Snow here can make it almost impossible to get into town for days. Sometimes weeks." Chance continued eating, not wanting to look into the eyes of his wife again. He was sure the fear was replaced with anger, but she needed to hear the truth about the weather.

"Surely not!" she exclaimed. "How do you manage then? What about your horses?"

"That's why the pantry is stocked full. And as for the horses, they are used to the winters." Chance stabbed a potato then slid it into his mouth. "I only need to make sure they stay near the pond and that they have access to the water."

"Blue wasn't born to live this way, was he?" Victoria's concern for his stallion gave him hope. "And how do you get water to the cabin? People weren't meant to be out in the middle of nowhere without—oh, you know what I mean."

"Once it snows, there'll be plenty of water just outside the door for cooking and bathing in," Chance continued, pushing his plate away. "We'll bring snow in by the bucket as we need it for cooking, washing dishes, as well as any other use we need water for."

"What!?"

Chance couldn't help but laugh at his wife. One look at the horror on her face and a person would never guess she grew up by the sea and along the docks of a busy port of call. Victoria was acting like a spoiled debutant, and he knew she was anything but. Well, a hopeful debutant at one time maybe.

"Look at it this way. When the sailors are out to sea and they need water, where do you think they might be able to get it?"

"Oh, I see what you mean now." She blushed, sipping her coffee. "Tell me about the ranch. And Blue."

Chance smiled. At least she pretended to be interested, very much like a well brought up lady. Maybe one day her interest would be genuine, but he didn't see that day coming anytime soon.

"There was nothing left for me at home after the war ended." Chance went on to tell her how he decided to get as far from the aftermath of the war as possible. So, he packed a few things and headed west until he reached Angel Creek.

He'd found his land one day out riding and knew in his heart this was home. Once he returned to town, he went into the Land Office and bought up a thousand acres, including some of the mountain range surrounding his property. He wanted to make sure he had enough room for a good size herd of horses. Even though cattle ranches were plentiful, there was a need for sure-footed horses and the mustangs provided that.

As soon as he had the cabin built, he started to find and watch the herds of mustangs until he chose several mares he liked. He staked out his land and built his fences.

"Once I settled on the mares, I already had a stud worthy of them. That's where your father came in. I purchased Blue and needed to get him from England to America. Your father had a ship in port in England. Once the ship docked in Wilmington, I got Blue and got ready to set out West. Then the war broke out.

"Without your father and that stallion, this ranch wouldn't exist. So, you see, I owed your father my life." Chance's words couldn't be any truer. Both Blue and Edmond had saved his life in different ways.

"So, to repay that debt, you agreed to marry me?" Eyes piercing through him, Victoria sat back in her chair.

Among other things. Chance nodded then said, "Yes."

VICTORIA WATCHED THE array of emotions roll across her husband's face until they stilled. His brows furrowed in thought. When her eyes met his, she had a feeling what he wanted to know. Everything.

The question left to her was how much was she willing to tell him? How much did he have a right to know?

"Why did you agree to the marriage?" As she suspected, Chance turned her question back on her.

Victoria thought about the request she'd promised to keep. Only the promise came before Papa took his own life. So really not much different than Chance's obligation to her father, she was bound by her word as well.

Except Chance hadn't heard the crack of the single gunshot explode behind a closed door. Or the sight of her father slumped back in his chair, blood pouring from the self-inflicted wound.

Victoria swallowed the sour bile surfacing in

her throat.

"I made a promise to Papa before he died," she said, blinking back tears on the fringes of her lashes. "And there was nothing left for me by the time the carpetbagger bank confiscated the shipping business and its accounts, as well as the home Papa still owed the bank money for.

"They said Papa was a traitor. A ship runner. The Yankees seized everything they could get their hands on. I didn't have anything left. No one to turn to. I couldn't even buy a loaf of bread."

Victoria let the tears fall for the first time since the day her father was buried. The burden lessened on her soul, but not on her heart. The break was still there, as fresh as the first crack months ago.

"I'm sorry," she said, wiping her tear-stained cheeks. "I'm not one to cry or show weakness of any kind. If you show your weakness, then they have you. Your business partners. Your competition. Your enemies."

"Crying is not a weakness, Tori." Much to his credit, Chance didn't treat her like a blubbering debutant. He didn't jump to his feet and rush over to console her. He looked at her as an equal. "Only a strong person will show their vulnerable side. There's no shame in it."

His smile soothed her in an unexpected way. Her husband, a man who didn't know a thing about her, apparently knew more about women than she would have guessed.

"How did you become so wise?" Victoria stood, gathering up their supper dishes.

"War teaches you things about life." That was

all he said before coming up behind her. "Tori, let me clean up tonight. You've had a long day, and so much has changed for you."

Victoria turned into him. She didn't dare look up into his eyes, fearful she'd turn into a blubbering mess. His effect on her, in his arms, was offsetting to her. Her hands pressed against his chest for a brief moment then she stepped away from his allure.

"Thank you, I think I will." She walked quickly across the room and up the stairs. Her heart raced with each step she took until she reached the safety of her room and closed the door behind her.

CHANCE STOOD OVER the sink, listening to Victoria's retreating steps. The bright starry night sky did little to the shock of what she'd told him. A chill ran through him. He walked over to stoke the logs in the fireplace.

If Chance had known the extent of the situation, he would have gone to Wilmington himself and brought both Victoria and her father back with him. He would have offered Edmond a small partnership in the ranch until he found a way to start over again. He could have courted Victoria instead of feeling obligated to marry her.

Helping Edmond would have been one thing, but courting Victoria? Is that what he really wanted to do?

Court his own wife?

Sitting in the rocking chair, Chance thought about it. Should he put the effort into winning over his wife or not? He only had a few weeks to convince her they could be good together. A partnership would benefit both of them. Would she agree to it? Could he agree to it and still keep his distance?

What choice did he have? He wouldn't send her back to a lonely and empty life. No amount of money could buy happiness or safety.

He'd learned that from the war.

The home he'd once had hopes of taking over was a casualty of the war. His family gone with it as well.

No, not completely gone. He had a wife now. And hope for the future.

Now, if only he could convince Victoria that the future was together, not apart.

But how? He didn't think the hearts-and-flowers routine would have any effect in winning her heart.

Unless she'd changed, and he doubted it, Victoria wasn't afraid to get her hands dirty. She'd loved the docks and working next to the men employed by her father.

If he was going to present their union as a partnership, then he'd have to treat his wife as just that. His partner.

And then maybe, just maybe, she'd trust him with her heart.

CHAPTER 7

*W*rapped in the quilt, Victoria stood gazing out the window. Sometime during the night, the snow had stopped, leaving behind a soft, glittering blanket of white, its loveliness marred only by the tracks leading to and from the barn.

"Humph, so he's an early riser," she mumbled, turning away. Yanking open a bureau drawer, she pulled on a pair of britches under the gown. Slipping the gown over her head, she reached for the red buffalo-checkered flannel shirt to wear. It was one of a few of her father's shirts she'd managed to rescue from the thieving carpetbaggers and faintly smelled of the sea. Thick socks kept her feet toasty warm as she walked across the cool floor.

"Let's see how he takes to his wife dressing like a man," she gloated, gathering her long tresses in a bun at the nape of her neck. Glancing around the room, she quietly made her way down the staircase.

The rich aroma of freshly brewed coffee floated toward her. It mingled perfectly with the faint sizzle of salt pork and eggs. Her tummy pinched, reminding her she hadn't eaten since supper last night.

"Good morning," she chirped with as much false gaiety as she could muster.

"Good morning, Tori."

His annoying nickname for her didn't bristle any less this morning than it had the night before. Why was it so difficult for him to call her by her given name? Maybe she should start calling him by his birth name and see how he liked it.

Oh, stop being so petty! she scolded herself, taking that last step off the stairs.

Chance stood near the stove, his profile giving her a nice view of him. He was ruggedly built and didn't have a paunch, which meant he was used to working. When he turned around, her heart leapt. The pulse in her neck sped up.

Frying pan in hand, his smile was as big as the Montana sky, his dimples as deep as the sea. The flannel shirt encasing his arms and chest defined every muscle as it rippled with movement. The dark jeans hung with ease around his waist and down his long muscular legs. The fit loose enough to work in, yet still sparked her imagination.

If only the situation were different, she sighed, unable to tear her gaze away from his manly splendor. The sound of him clearing his throat brought her gaze back to the amusement in his eyes. *Caught! Now what do I do?* She felt warmth blush through her from head to toe.

"I trust I didn't wake you." Chance placed a couple of plates full of food on the table. "I trust you slept well."

Victoria sat down, trying to keep herself from salivating over her plate. "Surprisingly, I slept like a baby for the first time in a while. I feel very refreshed and ready for a new day."

"Glad to hear it!" His eyes sparked with mischief, followed by a very sexy wink. What kind of trouble was she about to get into with his help?

Oh no! What has he got up his sleeve? And why do I have this sickening feeling I'm somehow involved in his scheme?

"You were up early enough this morning," she pointed out, sliding a piece of crisp salt pork into her mouth. Savoring the sweet and salty richness, she moaned with pleasure, licking the remnants of melted brown sugar from her lips.

Oh my! The man can cook. Really cook.

"I had thought I would have been up before you. I'll not make that mistake tomorrow," she said licking bacon grease from the corner of her mouth.

Sliding jam over a piece of bread, Chance chuckled. "I actually wanted to get an early start this morning. I need the wagon today, so I hitched up the horses after they ate."

"Oh? Where are you headed out this morning?" She smiled at him, reveling in the prospect of having the house all to herself for several hours today. It would give her time to inspect it and its contents more thoroughly. To learn more about the man her father trusted with her life.

"I'm glad to see you are dressed and ready to do a bit of work around here. It's refreshing to see a woman who's not afraid to don a pair of pants." His gaze, as true as his words, made her a bit disappointed that he approved of her outfit.

"If I offend you, I can always go upstairs and change," she said, finishing the last of breakfast and sipping on the cooling coffee.

"No, not at all. The way you are dressed is perfect for today." Chance rose and gathered the dishes, placing them in the sink. "I'll go get the wagon while you put on those boots and the heavy coat I bought you. I'll meet you outside in a few minutes."

"Outside?" she gulped, already shivering from the thought of the cold waiting on the other side of the door.

"Since we are temporary partners, I thought we should go out to look at the herd this morning together." Not waiting for her rebuttal, he walked straight out the door, pulling his coat up over his broad back and shoulders.

Victoria pursed her lips. The last of the cold air rushing in through the open door swept over her. She shivered slightly. From the cold? Or was it the prospect of being with Chance that made her do so?

"I've been outmaneuvered!" Victoria declared, tucking her pant legs into a pair of boots.

"HOW IN BLAZES am I supposed to keep my distance when she dresses like that?" Chance muttered, pulling his coat tighter around his chest. Trudging back to the barn, he hoped the cold, crisp air would cool the fire burning inside him. If he'd thought Victoria was an attractive woman when he first laid eyes on her, this morning she was so much more.

Apparently, she wasn't afraid of ridicule by putting aside the frills of a dress for sensible clothing. Clothing more fit for working ranch life. He laid odds she wouldn't shy away from hard work either. He counted his blessings she appeared different than when she was younger.

And she was his wife! A wife he couldn't kiss, let alone anything else. When she stepped into his vision this morning dressed in flannel and britches, he wanted nothing more than to take her in his arms and kiss her slow and easy.

The britches defined long, shapely legs she kept hidden under her skirts. The oversize shirt fueled his imagination on what was hiding underneath all that flannel. The opposite effect he felt she was aiming for.

"Any more mornings like this one, and I won't give a damn about our agreement!"

Chance climbed onto the wagon and eased the team of horses around the yard to the front of the cabin. He half expected to have to wait on Victoria; instead his breath hitched when she walked out onto the porch.

If she was trying to distract from her femininity, the effect was quite the opposite. The last thing he wanted in a wife was one who primped in front of a mirror all day. There was no time on the ranch for such nonsense.

She stood there with one of his winter hats jammed down over her head and earflaps hanging loose over her ears. A wool red scarf wrapped around the collar of the coat that was buttoned up to her chin. Her pant legs disappeared into dark boot shafts.

"You look—" He hopped down from the wagon, reaching her before she could take one step off the porch. Just because she wanted to dress like a man didn't mean he would treat her like one.

"The way I feel?" she asked, daring him to say what she really looked like. "Like a fraud?"

"You look ready for a long, good day's work, Tori." He smiled, took her by the elbow, and then guided her around the front of the wagon before she could protest. His hands slipped around her narrow waist, and he easily lifted her into the box. Even with all the winter garb on, she was light as a feather. He could feel her muscles contract from the pressure of his grip. As he suspected—not even close to being fragile.

He found every inch of her desirable—even in men's clothing.

"After the cold ride here yesterday, I wanted to be sure you weren't going to worry if I was warm enough or not," she quipped, settling onto the seat and pulling the blanket over her lap. "And I thought this coat would be warmer than the one you bought for me."

"No chance of that today," Chance chuckled, sliding in next to her. "I hope you had enough to eat. We may be out past time for lunch. I did manage to pack a few things before you came down this morning, though, so we won't go hungry."

"Oh" the only response from her. Chance

wondered if she really understood what he was saying or not. He knew having grown up in a city she had food readily available at any time. Out here, you took what you could with you and ate when you could.

"If all is well with the herd, we could be back in a few hours," he said, taking the reins in hand, urging the team forward. "If not, it could be several hours before we get back."

"Are you expecting a problem then?" she asked, a worried look flashing in her beautiful eyes.

"No, but I never know. I don't plan on anything beyond what is ahead of us, riding out to the herd." He shifted on his seat until he found the sweet spot that fit him perfectly.

The next few miles drifted with little conversation between them. The only sound was a hawk or two overhead, calling out to their mate. He loved the tranquility of the morning. It symbolized a fresh new day to get things right.

Did Victoria feel the same way? Or was she one of those women who needed to bustle about until the end of the day?

To SAY VICTORIA was disappointed her plan didn't work was an understatement. Of course, she'd been hoping for Chance to at least look at her in distain and tell her to go back upstairs and dress like a lady. Instead, the glint in his eye was quite the opposite.

He actually looked pleased! Any decent man would not have his wife dressed as I am, like a man.

Stealing a glance at Chance, she tucked the blanket tightly around her lap. He seemed to be a decent man. Unless all the attention since her arrival wasn't real. Impossible. She'd have sensed it. Seen some indication of an act.

"Would you ever give all this up?" Victoria asked, genuinely interested.

"No more than you would have given up your life in Wilmington if it wasn't absolutely necessary." Chance turned, meeting her gaze.

Sadness quickly passed through his eyes, and she immediately felt sorry for him. She knew how hard it was for her to leave her home. She couldn't imagine what it was like for Chance.

"I left my former life for this one by choice," Chance continued, turning his attention back on the snowy path they traveled on. "I haven't spent one day regretting it either. There is something about the crisp clean air here. There's a quiet peacefulness that soothes my soul. One day, it will yours as well, given the chance."

"I'm not so sure about that. However, I will concede it is awfully quiet, unsettling so for me." She missed the lapping of the water upon the shoreline and the sounds of a busy port.

"Unless you listen very carefully." Chance leaned in toward her, and she caught a whiff of horses and hay fluttering on the cold wind.

"I have been listening, and all I've heard is the sound of the horses and the wagon moving through the snow," Victoria said, hoping she didn't sound too cynical, but she wouldn't lie just to soothe his or anyone else's feelings. "Nothing for me to get excited about."

Chance stiffened as he turned to look at her.

"Oh, thank you for that. So, you're saying I am a bore to be around?"

"No, that's not what I'm meant at all," she stuttered, suddenly feeling overheated. "It's only, oh, I don't know."

"You don't have to explain, Tori. I understand." Chance reined in the horses and the wagon came to a crunching stop. "We're here."

Victoria's breath hitched in her throat. She'd never seen a herd of horses before. Yes, she'd seen them in the corrals but never out in the open. The sight before her was magnificent with the open range and mountains for a backdrop.

"They're beautiful," she remarked as the big black turned his head toward them, pawing the ground. She started to get down when Chance grabbed her arm.

"Wait for them to approach. Blue will be the first one to the wagon," he said, holding onto her with an iron grip. "They know my scent but not yours."

"And that matters?" she asked, surprised. After all, they were horses, not dogs.

"More than you know," Chance chuckled. "While Blue may be broken in and the mares tame, they live out here, free for the most part, and are wary of unknown scents."

Victoria nodded then settled quietly back onto the bench, her eyes on the small herd as the mares followed Blue slowly to the wagon.

Blue came round, giving her a snort. She froze, holding her breath. Then, as if by magic, the big black stallion blew softly against her face and nudged her gently.

"He likes you," Chance laughed.

"And that's a good thing?" Victoria asked, gazing into a pair of gleaming dark eyes. The horse's ears twitched back and forth before letting out a last puff at her face and turning away from her.

"From the horse's point of view, it's a start," Chance advised. "The hard part is gaining their trust. That's not so easy, Tori. They aren't pet dogs or cats. And they will run at the first sign of what they believe is a predator."

"And they all trust you?" Victoria realized as soon as the words were out how silly her question probably sounded to him. Of course, they trusted him. Why wouldn't they?

"Blue more than the mares, but they have come a long way over the past few years." Chance stepped down off the wagon, pulling a few carrots from his pocket. "I need to check on that black and white mare so stay in the wagon. I don't need to get kicked checking her teats. She may be having a foal earlier than I thought. I don't want her caught out in a storm while birthing."

Victoria nodded and watched as Chance trudged through snow toward the herd.

CHAPTER 8

"Whoa, girl." Chance slowly and quietly approached the very pregnant mare. "Easy, girl. I only want to see about your little one."

He ran a hand softly over her long, sleek neck, across her back, and down over her rump. Whispering to the mare, he looked under the swollen belly to see if her teats had begun to wax over.

"Dang it!" He stood, gliding his hand along her side as the foal inside moved. "I'm gonna have to bring you in, little lady. Just hold on a few more days."

Retracing the path his hand had previously taken, Chance offered the mare a carrot from the stash in his pocket. She really was a sweet little thing. He'd gained her trust quicker than the other mares, but that have been because she was so young when he first caught her.

"Well, little lady, looks like I'm gonna have to

get the barn ready for you sooner than I thought. That foal of yours is going to make an appearance real soon." He gave her neck one last pat then strolled over to check the other mares.

He was checking a blue roan when Victoria's scream echoed through the canyon. The roan crow hopped, knocking him off his feet as it ran off. Jumping to his feet, he looked toward the wagon. Blue had Victoria backed up against the back of the seat, his head buried into her side.

"Fool woman!" he hissed, running the best he could, slipping and sliding through the snow. He came to a screeching halt at the front of the wagon and laughed out loud.

"Should have worn your own coat," Chance chuckled. Blue had his nose glued to one of Victoria's coat pockets. He could see the horse's lips working to find that treat he was sure was hidden inside.

"Get. Your. Horse. Off. Of me!" Victoria demanded through the fear etched in her eyes. "I don't know what you think is so funny. Just get your horse away from me. Now!"

Chance came around Blue, looped his arm under the massive black neck, and grabbed a handful of Blue's black mane.

"Come on now, Blue," he said, giving the mane a tug and guiding Blue away from Victoria. "The lady didn't know that was a treat coat. I thought you had better manners than that."

Chance offered him the last of the carrots and led him back toward the herd.

"Don't pay any attention to her right now,

boy," Chance said, giving the stallion a piece of advice. "She'll come around. You just have to be gentle with Tori. You wait and see; she'll be fine in no time at all."

Blue nudged Chance in the arm as if saying he should do the same. Give Tori time to come to terms with her new life before throwing her into it head-on. And that's what he'd done only a few days after her arrival. Maybe he'd been wrong in trying to show her the beauty surrounding Angel Creek, but he didn't have much time to convince her to stay.

Did he regret bringing her out today? No. But next time he decided to try to convince her to stay, he wouldn't bring her back out here. He'd make a plea to her heart.

"All right boy," Chance chuckled, patting the long, sleek, black neck. "You win. I'll take it slow and easy, just like you do with your ladies."

Blue bobbed his head up and down then trotted off to his mares.

"If life were only that easy." Chance shook his head then turned back toward the wagon where his wife waited huddled on the seat.

"WHAT IS WRONG with me? I've never been afraid of a horse before," Victoria muttered, watching the interaction between Chance and Blue. They appeared so in tune with each other, and a hint of jealousy streaked through her.

Good God, I'm jealous of a horse! Not another woman, but an animal. Victoria shook the feeling away. She had no good reason to be jealous of anyone or anything. She was leaving in a few weeks. Yet she couldn't take her eyes off of the two of them. She couldn't stop her heart from beating warmth through her.

Chance had a calm and gentle manner with the massive stallion. And Blue followed along beside him like a well-trained dog. Any fool could see the respect, and dare she say love, the two had for each other.

She'd never had that before in her life. A kind of easiness with another being. Yes, there'd been respect and love with her parents, but it didn't seem the same somehow. What she witnessed between her husband and his horse was totally different and undefinable.

What would it take to get even an inkling of that admiration in Chance's eye for her? And why should she care? She wouldn't be here long enough for it to matter.

Or would she?

As tempting as it may be to just settle into a new life, she had her father's beloved shipping business to reclaim. Trying to win over a husband not of her choosing and one who'd so readily agreed to her terms wasn't worth all the trouble. If she were to live her life in misery, she might as well do so back home.

Still, as she watched him stroll back to the wagon, she couldn't help but wonder if she'd been too hasty in her proposal. Had her bitterness for the bankers clouded any reasonable judgment she made? She had to trust her father's decision to marry her off to someone she didn't know.

Then why didn't she trust Chance? Or herself?

Chance walked toward her with the ease of a man who knew exactly who he was. Yankee or not, there wasn't a cruel bone in his well-built body.

"I'm sorry Blue startled you, Tori." The wagon rocked slightly under his weight as he climbed up next to her. "I have had a little talk with him, and I don't think it'll happen again. At least, not until you ask him to approach you."

"You had a what with him?" Victoria asked wondering if he was serious. Just when she thought she'd been overreacting, her gentle husband showed to be a crazy coot instead.

Has he totally lost his mind, talking to a horse as if it was a person who would understand? There is no doubt that I am right in ending this so-called marriage sooner rather than later.

"A talk." Chance took up the reins, looking at her. "I know it sounds crazy, but that horse understands more than most human beings sometimes. Any cowboy worth a grain of salt will tell you the same thing."

"I think you've been out here alone for too long," she said, scooting as far from him as she could get without actually getting down from the wagon. "Animals do not understand what people say or think."

"You'll change your mind if you are here long enough." Chance slapped the reins across the team's rumps then turned back the way they'd come.

"Blue is extraordinary. He has a sense that I've never seen in any horse before. And believe me, I've been around a lot of horses in my life," Chance remarked.

"Well that, Chance Turner, remains to be seen." Victoria believed she'd married a lunatic. All the more reason to get through their agreement and get on the first boat back to Wilmington. At least there she knew what she would be facing—damn Yankees!

Here, she could wake trussed up in a box heading to God knew where.

Any thought of her marriage to Chance working out was gone. The spark of sadness surprised even her.

THE TRIP BACK to the ranch was quiet—deathly quiet. It was one thing to be out on the range alone, another being with your wife. Two strangers still trying to find some neutral ground on which to live their lives together. No matter how short the time together may be.

Chance didn't care for all this tension as thick as morning fog between them. Was it caused by something he'd said or done? Looking back on it, he didn't think so. He'd been gentle about her reaction to Blue and the possible consequences.

There was only one possible reason: Victoria was afraid of horses. How was he to know she was scared to death of horses? If she didn't want to talk about it, then she'd just have to sit and listen. A rancher's wife afraid of livestock wouldn't do either of them any good.

He had to get it off his chest or the next time, if there was a next time, she could get hurt. Or worse, killed.

Chance pulled up next to a small grove of Ponderosa pines. Once the team was tied off, he reached behind the bench for the saddlebag containing the food he'd stashed earlier this morning.

"Why are we stopping?" Victoria asked.

Judging from the tone of her voice, she was none too pleased, but he didn't care. They needed to settle this between them.

"Don't know about you, but I'm hungry." Chance pulled out two hand pies, passing one over to Victoria. "And this is the perfect spot. The trees block most of the wind, and the sun will provide some warmth while we eat."

"Thank you." Victoria took the pastry with a gloved hand, peeling back the paper wrapping. "This is something we could have eaten without stopping though. I'd like to get back to the cabin. I've had about enough of wide-open spaces and the horses who live there."

"Speaking of which…," Chance grabbed the opening while he could. No telling how quickly a woman would change the direction of a conversation.

"If you are going to lecture me on what happened out there, save it," Victoria snapped.

"What I have to say needs to be said." Chance reined in his frustration. "If Blue wasn't the horse that he is, he may have stampeded the herd when you screamed. The mare I was checking could have gotten hurt. In fact, I may have been kicked in the head.

"Lucky for you, that stud has been through

much worse than a silly woman screaming at him for nosing around her coat pocket."

"Silly woman? You cannot possibly be calling me a 'silly woman,'" Victoria spat, her brown eyes brewing like a pot of hot coffee.

"I am, and you were just that," Chance countered, the timbre in his voice shaking. "You could have gotten hurt if he'd reared and those powerful hooves came down on you. Not to mention—"

"Well, if that's the way you feel, then don't ask me to go with you next time. Why not just send this 'silly woman' back to her home?" Victoria glared at him as if it were his fault for asking her to go with him. "I'm sure you must miss your solitude."

"Dagnab it, Tori!" Chance growled, the last thread of his patience about to snap. "I am only trying to prepare you for the next time."

"You talk as though there will be a next time," Victoria snarled back at him. "If you think for one minute that I am ever going to come out here again, Mr. Chauncy Turner, you are sadly mistaken!"

Chance looked at Victoria, and knew that somehow, he'd lost control of the conversation. It was him who was being chastised for doing something wrong, not her.

"Fine! Then you can spend what little time you have left at the ranch alone"—Chance picked up the reins, snapping them across the horses' rumps—"Mrs. Victoria Turner!"

"Move on!" he hollered, feeling the frustration flow through his body to the reins. And that's just what he'd do. Move on, as if Victoria wasn't his wife.

That suited him just fine!

CHAPTER 9

ays after the incident with the horses, Victoria stormed around in the kitchen and pantry like a bull in a china shop. She had more flour on her face and apron than in the bowl.

She'd hardly seen her husband since they'd returned from checking the horses. And that was three days ago!

She should be happy Chance kept his distance. After all, it would make things easier when she left. And she wanted to leave, so why was her heart hurting?

He rose early, made coffee, and was out the door as Victoria came down the stairs. He'd be gone for hours on end, missing meals she took the time and care in preparing.

Then last night, he didn't come back in until long after she'd retired for the night. At least he'd eaten the bowl of stew she'd left warming on the stove.

Life grew lonely the longer Chance avoided her.

"If he thinks for one minute that I'm going to apologize for that day so he'll talk to me, he is sorely mistaken," she muttered, kneading her frustration into the bread dough with vengeance. "I don't have anything to apologize for. I wasn't the one pushing my nose into that darn coat pocket.

"Who expects a 'wild' horse to walk up to them and stick their nose into their coat pocket?" Victoria sighed, wiping an unexpected tear from the corner of her eye. "Even though the horse didn't bite me. He was only looking for a carrot he was used to finding there. Why would Chance blame me for being taken by surprise?"

Maybe she'd overreacted a smidgen. And maybe Chance had every right to lecture her. Even so, it didn't explain him not speaking to her since then except to say he'd be out in the barn working when they saw each other.

Has he washed his hands of her?

"What does he do out there all day? The only horses are the two that haven't left the paddock for days. I can't imagine it would take all day to care for two horses."

An image of Chance preparing one of the stalls to be lived in until the end of their agreement stabbed at her heart. "No!" Her breath hitched in her throat.

"He wouldn't do that." Fear, doubt and remorse mixed with her wild imagination. She had to do something but what?

Forcing the dough into the bread pan, Victoria placed it into the oven. She loved the buttery smell of bread baking; it always made a house feel like a home. Maybe it would remind Chance that this was his home. Not the barn.

"Not today. I'm going to find out just what is so darn captivating in that barn that he feels is more important than me!"

Wiping her hands with the bottom of the apron, Victoria grabbed her heavy coat. She'd see for herself what that husband of hers was up to.

Shading her eyes from the brilliance of the morning sun, she shuffled through the light snow covering the ground to the barn. She barely noticed the bite of winter in the air, her determination for the truth keeping her warm.

Reaching the barn, she took a deep breath then pushed open the door.

"Close the door behind you!" Chance called out from somewhere inside.

Closing the door, Victoria turned into the wall that was her husband's chest. Looking up, her eyes locked with Chance's. Her hands were plastered against his chest. Her heart thumped fast and hard. A prickly heat soared through her, and she quickly stepped away shaken by her response.

"Tori, what are you doing out here?" Chance asked, surprise then suspicion etched on his face. "Is something wrong?"

"Um, well," she stammered, looking for the right words to ask if he was moving out of the cabin and into the one of the stalls. "Well, to be honest, you haven't spoken to me in days. You spend all your time out here. I wanted to see what you were doing that was so important that you were avoiding me."

A high-pitched neigh from one of the stalls grabbed her attention. Curious, she walked toward the sound. The anger at Chance evaporated when small, black ears popped into view.

Inside stood the black and white mare Chance had checked on the other day. Her long-legged black foal with a wide white stripe down the center of his face peered at her. Its big, soft brown eyes seemed to see into her soul.

Her heart melted, and she instantly fell in love.

"Oh, he's beautiful," she exclaimed.

"*He* is a filly," Chance explained, his breath but a wisp of air across her ear. "A girl."

"This is what you've been up to?" She laughed, tears springing from her eyes. Relief flooded her. So, her husband wasn't making a place for himself in the barn. He'd been making a place for this baby and its mother.

"Yes, what did you think I was doing out here?" Chance asked, wrapping her in his arms.

The heat from him warmed her, and she felt herself lean into him. Would it be so bad if she stayed? Could she ever trust and allow herself to love Chance?

"Making a place for yourself," Victoria said in a hushed voice, her spine instantly stiffening.

"And why in all that is holy would I sleep out here when I have a perfectly good bed in a warm cabin to sleep in?" Chance loosened his hold on her slightly.

Please keep holding me close. Don't let go.

"Oh, I don't know. Because of me screaming like a banshee the other day," Victoria admitted, hoping she didn't sound as pathetic to Chance as she did to herself.

Chance laughed, swinging her around in his arms. She gazed into the heat of his eyes. Her body tingled. All control was gone. She leaned further into him.

She watched his mouth descend on hers until all she felt was his kiss. Slow. Easy. Hot.

"There, does that chase away that fear?" Chance asked, slowly caressing the length of her arms.

Victoria swallowed, shivered even as a blush warmed her cheeks.

"Yes, it most certainly does."

CHANCE GAZED INTO his wife's eyes. Whatever had possessed him to kiss her? If he'd made a strategic error, it didn't show on Victoria's face. Nor in her eyes, flickering like the flame of a candle. Passion that he had no right to have without permission.

The moment he stepped away, he felt her absence. A feeling he had no intention of ever feeling again, if he had anything to say about it. He couldn't take a chance on kissing her again; he may not be able to stop himself the next time.

"Um," he stammered, continuing to backpedal. "Have you started breakfast yet? I sure could use a hot plate of food when I'm finished out here. This little lady has had hers. Her momma and I worked hard to make sure she came into this world healthy."

Food! Why must my thoughts return to food all the time. Tori must think that's all I need her for— to cook. If she only knew I need, want, so much more from her.

"Oh no! The bread," she exclaimed, scampering out of the barn.

Slightly amused, Chance watched his city wife slip-slide across the yard to the porch and into the cabin. "That woman is going to be the death of me one of these days," he chuckled, closing the barn door to keep the wind out. "If she's around long enough."

That was it, wasn't it?

In the time since her arrival, he'd grown accustomed to her being here each and every day. The cabin that once felt like a place of shelter only now felt like a home. He didn't know how Victoria did it, but it even smelled different. Every corner held her light lavender scent.

He would have much rather been inside with her than in the barn with the horses. But he lived the life of a rancher, and he had a responsibility to care for his ranch. Including bringing in a very pregnant mare from the pasture and waiting for the foal to be born.

Most ranchers would have just let the young mare foal out in the pasture among the herd, regardless of the weather. After all, the wild mustangs seemed to fare well enough without human intervention.

No one in Angel Creek would ever think of Chance as being like most ranchers. When he'd first arrived with Blue, many questioned his sense in bringing an English-bred stallion in to breed to the mustangs. Even though his methods were unconventional, his mortality rate was one of the lowest. And his horses were some of the finest.

He hoped Victoria would come to understand and love his way of life. Away from the noise of a city. To live where the air was crisp and clean. Where people treated each other like family.

What if she didn't?

Would he trade it all for her love if she refused? He honestly didn't know, but he'd cross that bridge if he came to it.

VICTORIA RACED ACROSS the yard and burst through the door. Grabbing a towel, she swung open the oven door. Retrieving the bread, she breathed a sigh of relief.

The top wasn't nearly a golden brown. She hadn't burnt it after all, and it had a little longer to bake yet. She'd lost her head out there and panicked. Placing the pan back into the oven, she closed the door.

She ignored the sweet buttery aroma as she collapsed into a chair and stared at the open door. She didn't see the snow the wind blew in. Nor did she notice the cold snaking over her.

Her mind was elsewhere.

The barn where Chance had been preparing a stall for a newborn foal instead of avoiding her as she thought. He wasn't moving out of the cabin as her imagination led her to believe.

The kiss that took her breath away felt so right

and left her wondering about all the other things between a husband and wife. Things she'd never experience with Chance—her husband.

Chance, who proved to be a caring person to his horses, would be for her as well. He was tender and warm and desirable.

Which led her back to the kiss. Being wrapped in his arms. The insane wickedness that soared through her when his mouth captured hers.

What was she thinking, allowing him to kiss her? And God help her—she enjoyed the sensations it invoked.

The rush of heat.

The tingling running through her.

The desire for more.

More she didn't dare have or she'd have to give up her plan. If she gave in, she'd have no choice but to save her reputation and stay with Chance.

Chance. Her husband whom she willingly married with conditions. Conditions she insisted upon that, at the moment, seemed trivial and selfish.

But necessary, none of the less.

"I must stay the course," she said, shedding the heavy coat as she finally stood. "If I don't, my future independence will be lost. All that Papa taught me gone, if I give into the wants of my body."

Placing her coat on the peg, Victoria stood looking out the door. Across the yard to the barn where the man who sparked a flame in her worked.

"Not again," she declared, shoving the door closed.

Checking the bread one last time, Victoria

pulled it from the oven, setting it on the table to cool. The rest of breakfast could wait until Chance decided to come in from the barn—whenever that was.

After cleaning up the kitchen and discarding the floured apron, she went up to change clothes. She'd have to really beat the blue blouse and dark skirt to get all the flour out before doing any laundry.

Deciding comfort over propriety, she chose wool pants and the flannel shirt from the other day. Her manner of dress didn't seem to faze Chance either way so why not be practical. She wouldn't see anyone but him anyway so what did it matter how she looked?

Grabbing her favorite Jane Austin book she'd been reading once again, Victoria returned to the main floor. The fire gave off a cozy warmth. She settled into the chair next to the fireplace and turned to the page where she'd left off and fell asleep, reading about Austin's beloved heroine and unlikely hero.

A rush of cold air washed over her, sending gooseflesh up her body. She looked up. Chance stood at the door, brushing the snow off his shoulders.

CHAPTER 10

The sight of Victoria sleeping in the chair with an open book on her lap warmed Chance's heart. He stood in the open doorway, unable to take his gaze from her.

He imagined a baby, wrapped in a blanket, sleeping in her arms as she rocked slowly back and forth. He imagined she slept beside him, a crib next to the bed.

He imagined a life of love and happiness with Victoria.

The cold wind of winter blew through the door, reminding him that that life was not his to have.

"How long have you been standing there?" Victoria asked sleepily. "You're going to let all the warmth out if you don't close the door, Chance."

"Only long enough to brush the snowflakes from my coat." Chance closed the door then hung his coat on the peg next to Victoria's. "And I woke you, it seems. I didn't mean to do so."

"I only sat to read a page or two while the bread cooled. Before I knew it, you were standing in the door, letting the cold wind in." She smiled up at him with a sleepy little grin. A rush of heat travelled through him, and he wanted nothing more than to chase the cold away from her.

"Fresh bread always reminds me of home," Chance said softly, chasing away the melancholy feelings creeping into his heart.

Getting a knife, he sliced off two pieces of bread then joined Victoria by the fire.

"Would you like one?" He offered the larger piece to her, keeping the end of the bread for himself. It was his favorite part since he was a kid.

"Thank you," she said, setting her book aside. "Your mother, did she do a lot of baking?"

"Only when Cook was off, which was usually Saturday and Sunday." Chance ripped the bread apart, placing a piece into his mouth and moaning with pleasure. "I would say, if memory serves me right, as it has been sometime since I had any of my mother's baked goods, this bread is just as good, if not better, than Mother's."

"I take that as a high compliment." Victoria's eyes sparkled with happiness.

This was the first time he'd seen his wife relaxed and even the slightest bit happy. Had she turned a corner and was considering staying married to him?

"The book you were reading, who is the author?" Chance was genuinely interested. His missed the vast library he grew up with and the many adventures shelved there.

"Jane Austen," Victoria replied, caressing the worn leather cover. "It is one of her older novels, but I love the story so much that I never tire of it. Many may frown upon it because it is romantic, but I believe it is much more than that."

"Miss Austen was one of my mother's favorite authors as well. She would cry then laugh and sometimes even huff and puff each time she read her favorite one." Chance's heart pinged with both sadness and joy at the memory of his mother sitting near the fire each night and reading. Much how he'd found Victoria when he came in from the barn.

"Mother always said Miss Austen had a way of making you consider social standing and how irrelevant it is when it came to matters of the heart." Chance chuckled. "She was a romantic to the bone, and why she married my father is beyond me. They seemed so different from one another."

"Yet similar?" Victoria asked, echoing one of her favorite lines in the book.

"Yes, you could say that." Chance got up and put another log on the fire then went to cut himself another slice of bread. It really was better than his mother's and that said a lot.

"Do you read, Chance?" Victoria asked, pulling the blanket up over her lap.

"Yes, I do. And although my library isn't as vast as the one my parents had, I do have several more adventurous novels," Chance replied, returning to his place next to the now roaring fire.

"And who is your favorite author?"

"Jules Verne. Although it is a tossup really with Mark Twain," Chance said, crossing his legs casually in front of him. He was enjoying the conversation between them. It was easy. Dare he say comforting to know she enjoyed the same pastime that he did?

"Two different styles completely," Victoria remarked, obviously surprised by his choice.

"Yes, although both are thought-provoking. Mr. Verne takes you to places that may or may not exist in a way that does make one wonder if somewhere in the world they are waiting to be discovered.

"While Mr. Twain, much like Miss Austen, throws you into the fire of society and makes the reader see the good and the bad in our world. Miss Austen obviously wrote of life in England, while Mr. Twain concentrated on life in our own country.

"I have seen both worlds and while different, similar in many ways. Poverty isn't exclusive to one country or another. Neither is bigotry or the size of your bank account."

Chance shivered. He hated those memories when they crept into his soul. Memories of what his family had before the war and what they had now.

So, he really wasn't much different than Victoria after all.

THE SADNESS IN his eyes nearly broke Victoria's heart. What horrible thing could make a strong man like Chance go from a spark in his eye one moment to a shadow of darkness in the very next?

Maybe it was time she learned more about her

husband.

"What of your family? You don't talk about them, and it makes me wonder if they survived the war," she asked, surprised that her own painful loss surfaced for the first time in days. When had that incredible darkness begun to wane?

"Surely the North has fared much better than the South," she added, the assumption only going by her experience and what she'd overheard in her father's shipping office. Many a conversation centered around the reconstruction of the South. The Yankee carpetbaggers and the changes the old South must endure, however unpleasant.

"I will tell you my family is alive after losing most of their horses to the Union army." Chance's body grew stiff, and his face hardened. "My father and I didn't part on friendly terms when I came West. He felt I owed it to him to breed Blue to what mares he had left, which weren't many good ones. The army took the best of the herd.

"By the end of the war, I'd had enough with the hatred and devastation. So, I came here, made my own way and a home for myself.

"And although it wasn't in my plans, hopefully for you as well, Tori."

How was she supposed to respond to that? Chance had lost his family as well, only they were still alive while hers lay under the ground in a Wilmington cemetery. A loss was a loss, regardless of what it looked like.

Were they like Miss Austen's Elizabeth and Mr. Darcy? Different but the same?

Or was she allowing romantic notions to rule

over the reality of their union?

"Chance, you know how I feel and what I must do," she said half-heartedly. She didn't want to hurt him any more than he'd already been. Giving him false hope wouldn't do at all, and she couldn't be that unkind to him.

"Yes, about that." Chance glanced at her with questions darkening his eyes. "Are you sure there is something to go back to? Your parents are gone and so is the shipping business. What is there that draws you back to Wilmington?"

Victoria pondered his questions for a moment. What was there left for her there? Revenge? An eye for an eye and a tooth for a tooth? On whom and why bother, only to still be left penniless? She had no money with which to buy back the business. At least here, she'd have stability and companionship.

Yet wasn't it a matter of principle that she at least try to regain what should have been hers?

"The sea. The ships. The docks," she replied, her eyes moistening as she swallowed a soft cry. "I miss home and all that entails."

"This is, could be your home, Tori, if you'd only give it half a chance." Chance rose then walked over to the door. Shrugging his heavy winter coat up over his shoulders, he turned to her, saying, "I need to go check on the foal," then walked out the door.

The cold air washed over Victoria, waking her from the daydream of home.

"WHAT IS IT about that woman which infuriates me and excites me at the same time? Must she always be so determined to back to Wilmington?" Chance muttered, marching through the snow to the barn. "She has the right to know about the money. I know that. What a pickle you have put me in, Edmund."

He pushed open the barn door wide enough to slide through, then closed it behind him. The horses neighed their welcome, knowing they were about to have more hay to fill their bellies with.

"I must tell her, but not until she has decided whether or not to stay," he declared, tossing the horses two flakes of hay each.

"Tori has made it clear she doesn't wish to make a life here with me." He scratched the new foal between the ears. "What do you think? Should I give her the freedom she desires and let her run back to Wilmington emptyhanded? Or should I say nothing, and let her make her own decision between now and Christmas?"

The black filly bobbed her head up and down, her dark soft eyes laughing at him.

"You are correct, of course; let her make up her own mind when the end of our agreement arrives," Chance said, walking out of the barn and closing it up against the cold wind.

He walked quietly across the front porch and peeked through the window overlooking the kitchen. Tori worked methodically over the table filled with food, pans, and a kettle.

The roast beef he'd had stored was chopped into cubes along with enough potatoes to feed a family. He heard the faint melody of *Silent Night* being hummed while she gathered the items into the pot.

How could he let someone like her go? He couldn't. Somehow, he'd convince her to stay and be his wife.

Gathering his courage, he stomped loudly across the porch and swung the front door open.

"Did you enjoy watching me from the window?" she asked, head down as she continued to chop carrots.

Chance chucked. "You saw me then. I thought I was being quiet."

"I saw your shadow as you moved away from it." She looked up from her task, a smile on her face.

Chance shrugged out of his coat and hung it up. He turned to watch her put together their meal. There was something about that simple task that heated his veins. Now he understood why his father locked everyone out of the kitchen when his mother cooked.

The sensation was exhilarating.

"Can I help you with anything?" Chance came up behind Victoria and looked over her shoulder at the neatly piled chopped vegetables. "I'm a pretty hand with a knife."

"You are, are you?" Victoria turned into him, her nose against his chest.

His heart raced, and the blood flow in his veins heated to near boiling. Gently, he ran his hands lightly down her arms then relieved one of her hands of the knife that was still there.

"Yes, I am." Gazing into her eyes, Chance searched for the smallest hint of desire. It took several long seconds before he detected a faint spark. Satisfied, he smiled and stepped around her to the other side of the table.

"So, what is ready to be chopped?"

The disappointment that flashed across her face about undid him. Was it possible his steadfast wife wanted him to kiss her as much as he wanted to?

CHAPTER 11

*V*ictoria stirred the meat and vegetable mixture simmering on the hot stove while Chance sliced the onions. The heat that ran through her body moments ago was now reduced to a slow simmer. She still felt the embers snap, crackle, and pop each time she glanced his way.

She'd have thought for sure he would have retracted his offer to help when she presented the onions. Instead, unlike her father, who next to never stepped foot into the kitchen, Chance had gladly peeled then sliced into the yellow orbs with the precision of an expert.

Continuing to stir the contents of the pot while Chance stoked the fire, she closed her eyes. Almost immediately, a scene played out in her mind.

Snow fell outside a frosted window. A tree decorated with homemade ornaments stood in a corner near the fireplace, filling the air with a fresh pine scent.

Chance stood over the table, dressing the Christmas turkey. Next to him, a young boy with hair as dark as Chance's listened intently to every word as Chance explained how to prepare a turkey and why he did what he was doing to the wild turkey to make it edible.

A woman stood at the stove, her back to them, humming a Christmas song. She turned slightly, revealing a tummy swollen with an unborn child.

Their eyes met, and Victoria caught her breath.

The woman was her!

Impossible! I am leaving for home in a few weeks. This isn't real. This isn't what I want.

Without thinking, she grabbed onto the hot pot handle, screaming in pain.

"Tori!" Chance was by her side in a split second, guiding her over to the sink. "Quick, cold water."

"I'm…I'm," she cried as her husband gently drizzled water over the already blistering palm.

"Shush. Sit and hold this cloth on your hand," he instructed, guiding her over to the table. "It'll take some of the sting out."

With the hands of an expert, he cracked open an egg over a bowl, separating the white from the yolk. He then added a spoon full of lard to the egg white, mixing it thoroughly into a poultice.

With a tenderness she'd seen him use on the mares, she watched him apply the pasty mixture slowly over the redness on her hand. His eyes never left her hand as he wrapped it in a strip of material that appeared out of nowhere.

"I'm sorry," Victoria apologized quietly. "I forgot. My mind had wandered, if truth be told. And I forgot about the pan being hot."

Be honest with him. Tell him what you saw, Victoria. Tell him you saw the future with him, here in this cabin that is home. Not alone in Wilmington without him.

"I have to finish cooking our meal," she said, standing on shaky legs, only to feel his arms around her, and she tottered. "You must be hungry."

"I will finish. You sit, and let the burn begin to heal." Chance smiled at her, worry marring his beautiful eyes.

"You've treated burns before," she stated as he turned to go to the stove, ignoring her observation.

"You got a good start on the stew before your unfortunate mishap. And this isn't the first time I've cooked, Tori." He chuckled, shaking his head. "I am perfectly capable of finishing what you started."

"Don't forget about the biscuits," she said, thankful that she'd at least had a good start on the stew before her mishap. But it wasn't her fault, not completely anyway.

The vision of the two of them as a family unnerved her. Having a family with Chance wasn't in her plan. Having a family of any kind wasn't in her plans.

Not now. Not ever.

No matter what her heart said to the contrary.

CHANCE STIRRED THE contents of the pot, then slid the pan of biscuits into the hot oven. *Where had*

Victoria's mind been? Surely, she must realize how hot that pot handle can become.

He'd seen his share of burns, growing up and during the war. His mother wanted to make sure he knew how to dress one if a doctor wasn't available. He'd learned several different poultices to make and had used more than one on several occasions.

Clearing and wiping down the table, Chance placed eating utensils in front of Victoria and then some for himself.

"Coffee is hot enough if you want some," he offered, returning to the pot of stew one last time before moving it onto a spot on the stove to keep it warm.

"Yes, that would be nice," Victoria said, trying to smile bravely through the pain he saw on her face.

"That will be painful for the rest of the day, and maybe into tomorrow." He set cups on the table, filling them with the hickory nut coffee. "I would discourage you from cooking for a couple of days. It will give the burn time to heal and not cause you any more pain."

"How am I supposed to cook our meals then?" she asked, using her left hand to awkwardly lift the coffee cup.

"I'll take care of that until you can. I did have to cook for myself before you arrived," Chance chuckled, pulling the biscuits from the oven.

"Of course. I didn't mean to imply otherwise," she said, embarrassment coloring her face in a delightful shade of dark pink. "I am not acquainted with many men who know their way around the kitchen, let alone do their own cooking."

"My mother taught me how to cook from an early age. She said one day I may need to do so. And she was correct," Chance said with pride. He loved his mother and missed her, but he had happy memories and those kept his love for her alive.

"And the tending to burns, did she also teach you that as well?" Victoria asked, the coffee cup in her good hand.

"Yes, and a good thing too, as I've burned myself more than once during my lessons in the kitchen," he chuckled, placing plates of the stew and biscuits on the table.

"Your mother sounds like a very wise woman," Victoria remarked clumsily, holding the eating utensil with her good hand as she scooped some of the meat onto it. "Thank you for the spoon."

"I thought since you burned your right hand that a spoon might be easier. And I didn't think you'd take kindly to me feeding you. Although I'd be willing to spoon-feed you if you'd like." He grinned, reaching for her biscuit and smattering it with butter. "You do take butter on your biscuits, I hope."

"I do, with a bit of honey sometimes," she said as if she hadn't heard his offer of help.

Her smile sent a jolt through his heart.

VICTORIA SAT NEAR the fireplace feeling completely helpless but content. The blanket Chance had draped over her lap kept her legs warm as she watched him across the room. She had a perfect view of him clearing away their dinner plates and then scraping the remainder of the stew into a container for tomorrow.

He stood at the sink, a towel slung over a shoulder and shirt sleeves rolled up just pass his elbows. The muscles in his forearms flexed with the motion of washing dishes then drying them.

The longer she was around him, the more she felt her resolve to leave lessen. Each day, she had to remind herself she had to avenge her parents and take back what was rightfully hers.

If that was what Papa wanted, then why did he make me agree to marry Chance? Have I been wrong in believing my place is back in Wilmington and not here in Angel Creek? If I went back, I'd be alone. Here, at least, I'd have his company and his protection.

The question remained—was leaving worth the risk of knowing what she'd be leaving behind. Of that, she wasn't sure anymore.

"Are you warm enough, Tori?" Chance crossed the room, unrolling his sleeves and covering his muscular arms. "I could warm the coffee if you'd like some."

"Thank you, I'm perfectly content." She smiled at him, surprised she felt exactly as she'd indicated. She did feel content—and even a little bit happy.

Even though she hadn't been here very long, she was beginning to feel a bit settled.

"Well, that is good to hear. I would hate to think all my caring has not had some impact on you." Chance sat in the chair on the other side of the fireplace, his long legs stretched out in front of him. He looked relaxed and at home.

Several minutes passed in comfortable silence. Glancing over at Chance, Victoria admired the length of his body stretched out in comfort. His eyes were closed and his breath steady as if he were fast asleep. The slight smile on his face made him look younger than his years. Much like the little boy in her vision.

She shivered. A warmth snaked up her spine.

"Does it get very cold here, Chance?" she asked, not knowing what else to say. She didn't want to sit with him without conversation; it didn't seem polite for her to do so any longer. And the longer she looked at him, the more she saw that little boy.

"Yes, it can get very cold. And once the snow falls, we will be unable to go anywhere," he replied, his eyes still closed but the smile on his face widening.

Her stomach quivered, and her heart thumped. "Not even to town?"

"Not even to town," he said, opening his eyes and looking at her. "I will have to tie a rope to the barn so that I can make my way to it in a storm. I don't want to get lost in the snow when I go to feed the horses and have you find me frozen to death once it stops."

"It snows that much?" she gasped, haunting visions of finding him as the snow melted. "And you are right, that is certainly something I would like to avoid."

"Does that mean you are reconsidering the agreement between us?" Chance sat up in the chair, his hopeful gaze on her.

What had she just said? Did she say anything that would give him that impression? Surely not.

"I...I," she stuttered, trying to think of the words and how she'd used them. "I think I am tired and would like to go up and retire."

She got up from the chair, folding the blanket across the back of it. As she quickly walked toward the stairs, she heard his footfalls closing in.

She turned and was surprised to see the grin on his face. "Was there something you needed before I went up?"

Chance laughed, his eyes sparkling with joy. "No, but I do believe that you are going to need some assistance," he said, nodding toward her bandaged hand.

"Oh, yes, of course, thank you." She turned away, butterflies fluttering in her tummy as she forced herself to walk slowly up the stairs to her room.

Thank goodness Chance had seen fit to grab a lantern, as she had forgotten it in her haste to escape to her sanctuary. Chance was only a few steps behind her, and she forced herself not to run ahead and slam the door behind her.

Approaching the landing, Chance stepped around Victoria and into her room. She stood in the darkened hall, wondering what she should do. Should she wait and see if he lit the lantern in her room? Or was she supposed to follow him into the darkness of her private room?

Another soft yellow light was her answer.

Her breath hitched when she stepped into her room. The glow of the two lanterns cast romantic images across the room. The flames flickered off the walls, casting a magic spell.

"I'm not sure how to do this without—" Chance said, his gaze sending hot shivers through her.

"You'll have to keep your eyes closed." She swallowed, her heart pounding just under her undergarment. "Do you think you can do that?"

"Yes, as best I can," he replied, setting the lantern in his hand beside the one of the bureau.

They met at the end of the bed where her nightgown lay neatly across it. Victoria turned her back to Chance, holding her breath.

Anticipating his touch.

His arms came around her. At first, his fingers fumbled with the buttons on the flannel shirt but then quickly found a rhythm. She felt the soft material slip over her shoulders and down her arms, where he gently tugged a sleeve over her bandaged hand.

Reaching for her gown, she tried to slip it over her head one-handed. Then she felt it.

His hands taking the cotton gown from her hands and slipping it over her head. She turned and was enveloped in the warmth of his arms before she could take another breath.

Their lips met, and she heard herself moan against his mouth. She wrapped her arms around his back, leaning into him. Giving herself to him.

Almost.

She stepped out of his embrace. When she looked up, a smile brightened his face. Desire burned in his eyes.

"The way I see it, you have two options, Tori. You can go ahead and sleep in those britches. Or you can let me take them off of you," he said, stepping away from her. "I leave the decision up to you."

Victoria thought for a moment, contemplating how uncomfortable sleeping in the pants would be. And whether or not she could trust herself if he helped her out of them.

"I think," she said, licking her bottom lip. "I think I'd like some help with them. If you promise to be a gentleman."

"I can make no such promise, Tori. So, the decision is up to you."

"Yes, please," Victoria whispered as she closed the small gap between them.

Chance nodded then slowly unbuttoned each button until the pants slid down her legs and pooled onto the floor. He pulled back the blanket and quilt then swept Victoria into his arms and gently laid her on the bed. Her body hummed in anticipation.

"Good night, Tori," he said, walking over to douse one lantern and picking up the extra one before leaving her alone in the dark.

CHAPTER 12

antern in hand, Chance paused at the top of the stairs and furrowed his brow in thought. Had his wife just made a suggestion to him? Or was she only testing his integrity?

Either way, he may have failed miserably as a husband not knowing for sure what she really wanted.

He knew what he wanted. He wanted Tori to be his: body, heart, and soul. Completely and fully. If he didn't have all three then he'd have to find a way to work through the frustration.

Jogging quickly down the steps, Chance checked the fire as it burned low. Once he was satisfied it was burning itself out, he then returned to his room.

The moment he closed the door, he felt an emptiness he'd not noticed before. He'd grown accustomed to imagining sharing the space with his new wife in the months before her arrival.

He'd pictured her arrival much differently than it had been. He'd thought they'd be married without any conditions. He'd imagined her joy to know, even though married to him, she'd still maintain her own source of finances and her independence as well.

None of that came to be a reality. Instead, he'd agreed to a "trial period" to see if they were compatible. So, he made the decision to wait to see if Tori was going to stay or leave before giving her the bank account that would afford her the ability to live in comfort all of her life. Wherever she chose.

If not alone as well.

If there was any hope of her choosing to stay for the right reasons, the only thing he could do was tell her about the money her father left her. He'd write her a note, place it and the bank account information on the table, then head out to bring in the other mares with their foals.

Picking up the writing desk, Chance dipped the pen into the inkwell and began.

"My dearest Tori…"

VICTORIA ROSE WITH the sun shining and snow falling just outside her window. The faint tracks leading from the house to the barn where barely visible. Once again, Chance was up, and chores completed before she opened her eyes. She was going to have to get better at this if she stayed on as his wife.

She stepped out of her gown and into the shirt and pants that lay neatly on the chair next to her bed. Careful not to disturb the bandage on her injured hand, she successfully managed to get herself dressed.

Her heart raced as she looked out the window once more. She couldn't wait to get downstairs and see her husband.

Husband? she questioned then laughed.

"Yes, Chance is my husband. And I couldn't do any better," she confessed aloud, slipping her feet into her shoes.

She'd lain in bed during the night, thinking of her gentle man. Not once had he pushed himself upon her when he had ample opportunity to do so. His gentle touch fueled something in her she'd never felt before.

Could it be love?

A glorious feeling of attraction she could never deny.

It was time to tell Chance she was going to stay in Angel Creek with him. She couldn't wait to go downstairs and tell him she was his—if he still wanted her.

"Chance?" Victoria called out, jogging down the stairs. Looking around the empty cabin, her joy sank.

The cabin felt unnaturally quiet. The smell of coffee was faint. The crackle of the fire even more so.

Victoria stood in the middle of the large open living area, scanning everything slowly. Then she noticed his hat, heavy coat, and warm boots were gone. As her gaze moved farther around the room, she then saw it.

On the table, leaning against a coffee cup, an

envelope with her name scrawled across it. Her heart sank until it landed on the floor beneath her feet.

A chill soared through her. Not sure if it was from the cold in the room or the obvious message from Chance, she stoked the fire, adding more logs to the hearth.

Making a wide berth of the table where the message waited for her, she looked out the window toward the barn. Any evidence leading to or from the building was completely covered by the falling snow.

A rope adorned with strips of cloth was tied around the porch railing, stretching out toward the barn, hadn't caught her attention from the bedroom window. Then she remembered Chance saying he did that when a good snowstorm looked to be brewing. Judging from the graying sky over the mountains, one was definitely brewing.

"Where have you gone, Chance?"

Victoria turned from the window, her gaze falling immediately on the envelope. She couldn't avoid it forever.

Breathing deeply to steady her nerves, she grabbed it from its perch and took a seat next to the fireplace. The thickness surprised her. Ripping it open, she unfolded the parchment containing her husband's words to her.

My Dearest Tori,

Do not worry. I have gone to bring the rest of the herd closer to the homestead and to bring the other mare and her colt to the barn. The weather will be taking a turn, and I must be sure the horses are safe and have plenty of food and access to water.

I have taken provisions in case I am delayed in my return. If all goes well, I will be home before nightfall, if not shortly thereafter.

My time away will give me the opportunity to decide if you were entertaining the idea of changing your mind and are staying as my wife. Last night gave me hope that you have done so.

However, I cannot rejoice at the prospect in good conscience. There is something you must know before you agree to stay, only to regret it later after all has been exposed.

Enclosed is a bank ledger. You will notice it has your name, and your name only, on it.

Victoria's stomach lurched in an unladylike manner. She found the ledger and gasped.

As Chance had indicated, her name was at the top as sole owner of the account. The date on the paper from the Angel Creek Bank was several weeks before her father had taken his life.

The total in the amount column was enough to buy back the shipping company!

"This is a fortune!" she whispered, tears racing down her cheeks and her mind spinning with questions. "And Chance knew all along. Why would Papa send this amount to him and not save our home, at the very least? Papa said all was lost, made me promise to marry a man he sent the money to, then took his own life. Why?"

Victoria looked over the ledger closer. Other than the deposit entry, there was no indication of any withdrawals.

Of course, once she married Chance, her money had become his.

"He only wanted my money, not me," she cried, storming up the stairs, the letter and ledger fluttering to the floor—forgotten.

COAT COLLAR UP tight around his neck, leather buckskin gloves protecting his hands, Chance rode into the blizzard, keeping his hat pulled low over his eyes and a kerchief covering his nose and mouth. The brutal wind slung ice crystals against his exposed skin.

He may have not found the herd if not for Blue's midnight color. As luck would have it, old Blue was already heading the herd toward home when Chance came upon them.

But now the going grew slower, and before long, the sky would begin to darken. If the weather didn't let up some and he couldn't make up any time lost, he'd be bedding down in the shelter of the pines. A plan he'd been prepared for but hadn't thought he'd need to use.

Since leaving the cabin as the sun rose above the horizon, Victoria was never far from his thoughts. The memory of her essence imprinted on his mind. The heat of her skin against his fingertips as he removed her clothing last night kept him warm.

But it was her beautiful face that kept him moving toward home. He'd never really considered the cabin home before. These past few weeks living with Victoria had turned the cabin from a place to live into a home.

He knew she'd have found his letter explaining the ledger by now. How had she taken the news that she wasn't as desolate as she'd thought?

Not well, he imagined. Probably was pacing the floor, waiting for him to walk in so she could give him a good vocal thrashing. Then she'd pick up her bags and try to head to town, blizzard or not.

On the other hand, had his words of love helped to soothe her anger any? Or the promise that her inheritance was all hers, that he wanted none of it a balm to her ire?

If he knew his wife at all, she hadn't gotten as far as his confession. Once she'd read about and seen the ledger, she would be furious. Then befuddled as to why her father would do such a thing to her.

Then ultimately wondering if he'd agreed to marry her to get his hands on her money. Even though his letter indicated otherwise.

He didn't need her money; there was plenty of his own in a bank back East if he wanted it. Thankfully, he hadn't and didn't plan on going into that account for any reason. He'd made his own way, and he'd keep doing so.

Without his family's money. Or Victoria's.

Spotting a grove of trees, Chance gave a double trill whistle. Waiting for Blue's response, he turned his mount toward the pines. He heard the black gather the mares and move them near the pines as well. It would be far too dangerous for the herd to shelter inside the grove, but Blue would keep them close enough during the night.

Having found a place suitable enough for a fire, Chance settled in with some jerky and coffee then huddled under a makeshift shelter from the wind and snow. He knew by morning's light the snow would be deeper, but he hoped the wind and snow would have stopped long before the sun rose again.

Exhausted from fighting the wind and cold, Chance closed his eyes and soon fell asleep to the music of a Montana night.

CHAPTER 13

Victoria woke curled in a ball. The room was cast in shadows from the setting sun. She shivered against the cold seeping into her bones. How long had she been asleep? Surely not most of the day!

Her eyes felt swollen from crying. Her muscles resisted her attempt to straighten her legs out. And her heart was broken all over again.

Next to the bed sat the travel chest she'd dragged out from the hallway into her room. Then she remembered, the anger taking over when she'd run up the stairs.

Chance's letter. The bank ledger. The secret.

She refused to stay a day longer than necessary in this cabin with a man who kept such things to himself. Especially those that concerned her. Important ones that would change her life.

"How could he not tell me about something this important?" she hissed, tossing clothing into the chest. "He knows how important it is for me to make my own way. To take back what was rightfully mine."

To depend on no one but herself.

"And to think I was going to tell him I changed my mind. That I was going to stay here, with him." Victoria plopped back down onto the corner of her bed. Tears trickled down her cheeks. The dark feeling of immense sadness and loss began to creep back in. "I started to trust him."

"I will NOT fall victim again to my circumstance," she vowed, shaking the darkness away.

Her father had given away her independence when he sent the money to a man she didn't know. A man she'd agreed to marry hours before her father took his own life.

Why? Why would he do any of that? What was he hoping to accomplish?

There was only one person who had the answers. And he wasn't here.

Abandoning the haphazard packing, she left the room and jogged down the stairs, her mind racing in confusion.

While her heart begged her to stay, her head demanded otherwise.

"Where is that darn letter?" she whispered urgently.

Reaching the bottom of the stairs, Victoria frantically searched the room. Nothing on the table but the cup where the envelope had been propped.

Feeling defeated, she sank onto the bottom step, head cradled in her hands. She had to stop the panic threatening to overtake her.

She had to find the letter, but more importantly, the ledger. The ledger was all the honesty she had in her life. The ledge was her way to financial freedom.

"Think, Victoria," she muttered, lifting her head. She opened her eyes. There on the floor to the left of the staircase was the ledger, the letter less than a foot away from it.

Breathing a sigh of relief, she gathered the papers then added a log to the fire. Sitting in the chair, she scanned over what she'd already read of the letter, surprised to find there was more.

I am sure you are very hurt and angry right now. Please understand I was only following your father's instruction—until now.

I could no longer in good conscience keep you from what is rightfully yours. If you are to stay as my wife, I want you to do so without any secrets between us.

I have come to care deeply for you, and my heart demands that if you do decide to stay and build a life here with me, then you do so on a foundation of honesty. Otherwise our life together will be a lie.

Please forgive me, Tori.

Affectionately yours,
Chance

Victoria swiped at a tear even as her heart sang in joy. If her interpretation was correct, it seemed her husband may be in love with her. No fancy words. No flowery poetry. Only honest words that touched her soul.

And her heart.

CHANCE GASPED THEN opened his eyes. Somewhere in the distance, the howl of wolves sang in the night. He heard the horses shuffling nervously in the snow.

Something was afoot. And it was more than the wolves. Climbing out from the shelter, he moved slowly in the night.

His saddle horse pawed the ground, straining against the tie down.

"Shush, big guy," he soothed, gliding a hand softly over the horse's neck.

Then he heard it.

The low growl. The high-pitched screech from Blue as the herd stampeded. Grabbing his rifle, Chance broke through the tree line, took aim, and pulled the trigger.

The cougar fell to the ground seconds before it would have sunk its claws into the young colt. Breathing a sigh of relief, Chance lowered the rifle and watched the herd run toward the ranch and out of sight.

"So much for a peaceful night," he muttered under his breath, trudging back to his campsite after making sure the cougar was indeed dead.

The snow was letting up, but it was still dangerously cold for him to break camp in the night. Instead, he relit the fire, placed the coffee pot on it, settled back under the shelter, and waited.

His thoughts wandered back to Tori, his letter, and the bank ledger.

Had he been selfish in leaving Tori to face his news alone? Or was it cowardice on his part in not wanting to see her full rejection of him?

On the other hand, if he hadn't been here, that colt would have been dinner for the cougar. With only its mother to protect it, the colt had been helpless.

Tori was anything but helpless.

And he loved her.

Loved her enough to set her free, if she so desired. His being away would give her time to decide her fate without any interference from him.

He'd given her back the power she'd had taken from her.

And he'd do it again if he had to.

VICTORIA SHUFFLED THROUGH the last pages of the letter until the ledger stared her in the face. The evidence of the truth in Chance's words—if she chose to believe them.

Line for line, she examined the bank document. The only name, and sole owner of the account, read: Victoria Montgomery.

The money had been deposited a month before her father's death. Proof of her father's plan to have her far from Wilmington.

Why? To start a new life with a man who would allow her financial security outside of his own? Her father had either been a desperate man or a genius.

Or a little bit of both.

She pushed out of the chair and walked to the window. A shiver of dread passed through her.

"Where are you, Chance?" she asked, her stomach upending inside. Something was wrong. She didn't know what, but she had the same feeling she'd get on the docks when a ship didn't come into the harbor on time.

If not for what moonlight there was reflecting off the snow, it would be pitch black outside. If she dressed warmly, she could get a horse ready and set out to find Chance.

She'd have to wait for the sun to come up first. Or did she? If Chance was in trouble, every minute counted.

Grabbing her winter garb, Victoria checked the fireplace, making sure it would burn itself out and not the cabin to the ground. Satisfied they'd return to their home in one piece, she dressed in layers. Stuffed her feet into boots. Pulled a hat with earflaps down over her head. Slipped into the heavy wool-lined coat and wrapped a scarf around her neck and face.

Stepping out the door, she pushed back against the cold wind threatening to knock her over. Finding the rope that led to the barn, she grabbed it with gloved hands and began the trek to the barn, holding tight to the rope guide.

Slipping and catching her balance several times, Victoria finally reached the barn door and gave it a shove. The heavy door slid open with some resistance from the snow but finally relented.

She was met with a whinny from the horses as soon as she closed the door. Not knowing how long she'd be gone, Victoria put several flakes of hay in the stalls and made sure the young mare and her colt had plenty of water.

Saddling the other riding gelding, she walked him outside, closing the door behind her. Stepping into the stirrup, she settled herself into the saddle.

Adjusting her cap and scarf, Victoria rode to the north. She prayed she was headed in the right direction. Two of them lost here in the snow would be disastrous.

She rode for what seemed like days. Feeling snow blinded as she approached the ridge, she blinked against the rising sun reflecting off the snow. Then she saw them.

The herd with Blue in the lead.

"Chance!" She cried out in joy at having found him, only to have it destroyed.

Only the herd thundered past her. Chance wasn't with them.

CHAPTER 14

His rifle at his side, Chance woke exhausted, as if he'd slept with one eye open all night. Maybe he had. He had been listening to every little sound. The last thing he wanted was any surprise visitors creeping in during the night. No telling if there was another cougar on the prowl looking for its next kill.

But now the morning sun's rays threw light through the pines, and he began to break camp. There was a good chance Blue and the herd were close to the ranch by now. At least, he hoped they were. If not, he'd probably catch up now that it had stopped snowing.

But what of Tori? Had she slept well? Or had she been up all night with a shotgun, planning the battle he was sure to have with her?

Not that he blamed her any. He'd be mad as

hell if the situation was reversed.

The money was a healthy amount that put her into the well-to-do category. High society back in Wilmington would once again welcome her with open arms. Suitors would be knocking down her door just to get an audience with her.

Nothing more than wolves howling at her door, and no one there to protect her.

Was he any better? He was not only at the door but inside as well.

"What have I done?" He jammed the wool horse blanket into a saddlebag then covered the campfire with snow.

"I have handed her over to them lock, stock, and barrel. Who is the bigger fool here? Me, of course. I've gambled on love and lost."

Tightening the cinch, Chance stepped into the stirrup, swung a leg over then settled into the curve of the saddle. Reins in hand, he urged his mount out of the trees and into the snow glistening valley.

With the wind now at his back, he kept his coat collar pulled up against the cold. He prayed it was colder outside then what may be waiting for hm back at the ranch.

An empty cabin? No, Tori wouldn't leave on her own without giving him her piece of mind. Or would she? Actually, he wouldn't put it past her to up and leave without giving him a chance to explain everything.

But what was there to explain? That her father saw the end coming and didn't want his little girl left completely penniless? Without someone to look after her best interests? Someone far from

Wilmington who he could trust?

Ha! Tori could very well do that herself. Chance saw that long before her father ever would have. Edmond saw only the little girl, not the strong grown woman she really was. As so many fathers before him, a heartbreaking mistake when finally realized.

If Chance ever had any girls of his own, he'd make sure they were strong of mind and body. Able to take care of themselves, whether they married or not.

That was unlikely to happen.

The only woman he wanted children with may or may not be home, waiting for his return.

AS LUCK WOULD have it, the snow had stopped falling. Victoria followed the herd's trail leading back to where she hoped to find Chance well on his way home.

Blue had whinnied "Hello" as she rode past the mares. No doubt letting her know she was headed in the right direction. At least, that's what she wanted to believe since she didn't know the stallion as well as Chance.

All alone on Chance's land, their land, she finally came to see the beauty surrounding her. There was a wildness, that while unlike the open water of the sea, she found soothing and comforting. And she immediately realized why Chance had called this place home.

If she understood that, it meant they were very much the same. Something her father had seen long before Reconstruction had invaded their once peaceful lives.

Here on the ranch and in Angel Creek, no one from that horrible place of chaos could reach her.

The only thing to have softened her resolve was the kindness Chance had shown her. Even the evidence of him having deposited her inheritance into the bank with herself the sole owner indicated an honest man. A man to be trusted.

A man with principles.

And she found love in her heart for such a man.

A man named Chauncy Turner.

A man she was married to and for the first time did not regret or want to end it.

Her horse bobbed his head and nickered. Looking from under the brim of the cap, she saw what appeared to be a lone rider.

Could it be? Her heart raced. Her body seemed to catch on fire.

She urged the horse forward through the deep snow. As reckless as it was to approach the rider not knowing if it was Chance or not didn't stop her.

"Chance!" she called out the closer they came to each other.

She noticed the rider's horse moving faster in her direction. She reined in her mount and slid out of the saddle.

Her husband was alive, and she wanted nothing more than to hold him in her arms.

CHANCE LOOKED UP as the rider came into sight. There was only one person who would be foolish enough to ride out after him.

Victoria!

Pressing his heels into horseflesh, the gelding moved at a quicker pace. The cold of the wind at Chance's back was replaced by the heat in his veins. She was still here. Tori hadn't left him—at least not yet.

If she were going to leave, he doubted very much she'd have ridden out to find him. She would have waited for him to return to the ranch.

"Tori!" he called out, dismounting and running through the snow toward where his wife stood.

As the distance between them closed, she ran to meet him. Picking up speed, he reached her, and they both came to a stop, gasping for air.

He waited, sizing up the moment.

He noticed the tears that stained her cheek.

Taking a step closer, then another, she flew into his arms, knocking them both to the ground. He looked up into her eyes and saw what his heart desired in them—love.

Then she kissed him, and he knew in that instant he was hers. Come what may, they belonged to each other.

"We need to talk," he said, rolling out from under her.

"You bet we do!" she exclaimed, getting up on her knees then standing.

He should have given her a hand and would have if not for the look of "don't you dare" on her face.

"There is something I mean to say to you," she began, brushing snow from her.

"Then say it before I do something I may regret," Chance threatened lightly.

She's not leaving. I can feel it in my heart.

"I have had time enough to consider what you have done at my father's request," she started, righting the slightly dislodged cap.

"You have? And what…" he started then closed his mouth when she scowled. This wife of his didn't want his interruption.

"I have, and if you'll stay quiet long enough, I'll tell you what I've decided." She took a step toward him, her gaze sending hot shivers up his spine.

"I cannot fault you for doing my father's bidding. I'm confident he had a good argument for it. What I can fault you for is not telling me to my face about the money."

She was now inches away from him. He wanted to take her in his arms and never let her go. But the time wasn't right—not yet.

"I also fault you for scaring me half to death before we are married for not even a mere month. I have no intention of becoming a widow until we have several great grandchildren running around on our land."

"In order for that to happen, you'd have to stay here on the ranch married to me." He closed the gap between them, fighting to keep his hands away from her.

"I believe that, Mr. Turner, is what I have said, is it not?"

"Are you ready to go home, Mrs. Turner?"

Victoria looked up at her husband, wondering how she ever doubted him. She had been so filled with mistrust and grief that she hadn't seen his generosity, and eventually, his love.

"Yes, Mr. Turner, I am ready," she answered, giving him a kiss on the cheek.

Chance snatched her in his arms and placed her in his saddle. The reins of her horse in his hand, he easily mounted behind her.

The beautiful snow-capped mountains came into sight, and she snuggled closer to the man who would be the father of her children. The man who healed her broken heart. The man who understood her.

The man she loved as much as he loved her.

THE END

Thank you for reading *Victoria (Angel Creek Christmas Brides, Book 17)*! I hope you will come along with *Meg (Angel Creek Christmas Brides, Book 18)* on December 18, 2020.

Meg Todd is tired of putting her happiness on hold. When she learns her bullying brother-in-law has horrifying plans for her future, she asks an attorney family friend for help escaping. Meg wants her own husband and home and is willing to move over halfway across the country to achieve her goal. Along the way she agrees to take two children for their dying mother. Is she too impulsive?

Curtis McClain has to be careful with his small savings or it won't fund his dream of his own newspaper. He wants a wife—he needs someone to help him with the newspaper. If he can combine the two, then he'll be all right. In a few years, they can start a family. But will a woman want to move to the middle of nowhere on those terms? Will she grow to care for him in spite of his reserved nature?

He is slightly annoyed when his wife shows up with two orphaned children. When he learns the amount of her inheritance, he decides she won't be content to stay with him. That is, until a terrifying event occurs. Can these four become the happy family of Meg's dreams?

Get your copy of *Meg* here:
https://mybook.to/McClain

BONUS EXCERPT

Red River Crossing

Men of the Double K, Book 1

CHAPTER ONE

Texas, 1887

The sun crept over the eastern horizon, giving birth to a new day. A gentle breeze ruffled the tall prairie grasses like ripples upon the river. He inhaled deeply. He would miss the tranquility that mornings had brought him these past ten years.

Morning was the best time of day. Before the rest of the world woke, one could contemplate one's reason for living that day. In those brief glorious moments, Beauregard Kennedy always knew being on the Double K alongside his brothers was his place.

But like the seasons, things change—and so had the Double K. He was the odd man out with no wife or children to call his own. No one's fault but his own. He even regretted it at times. This was one of those times.

Gulping down the last of his coffee, Beau took one last look at his and his brothers' land stretched out along the horizon then returned to his small, lonely cabin to pack the rest of his few belongings into his saddlebag. He'd never expected to resume the business of chasing outlaws, but when word from his old friend William Pinkerton came, he couldn't turn his back on the trouble.

Now that his brothers were settled, there really wasn't room for him on the Double K any longer. It was time for him to get on with life; he'd been scratching that itch far too long.

Beau took a final look around his silent cabin then walked back out to where his brothers waited for him.

"You aren't going to make this easy on me, are you?" Beau shook his head, looking at his brother Cyrus.

While Cyrus had found love twice in his life, Beau had grasped it once then let it go. Would his life have been different if he'd married Jess and brought her home with him to the Double K? Jessica Sanders was most likely living on Bowdoin Square in Boston as some high society man's wife by now as her father had planned for her all along. That was water under the bridge—it was too late for what might have been.

"Why should I?" Cyrus asked, a smirk on his face. "Easy has never been your way, Beau."

"I reckon you're right," Beau agreed, glancing around, hesitant for a brief moment. He was doing the right thing in heading back to Brokengulch where trouble waited to be found and resolved. He'd lived a safe life on the ranch all these years. He needed to be reminded why he'd given up the life of a hired gun for that of a rancher one more time before it was all over.

"Suzie sent this along for you. She'd have come herself but with another baby coming, she's an emotional mess." Cyrus handed him a bundle of carefully wrapped broadcloth. "There's jerky, biscuits, and a jar of Suzanne's famous apple butter to keep you for a while."

Beau placed the bundle carefully into his saddlebag,

nodding his thanks. He knew how uncomfortable his sister-in-law had become these past few weeks with their third child. There would be another addition to the growing Kennedy clan by Christmas.

"Uncle Beau." Johnny stepped forward, handing him a leather-bound journal and pencil. His nephew had become quite the storyteller under the guidance of his stepmother, Suzanne. Beau was sure that although Cyrus was proud of his eldest son, he probably wished Johnny's talents leaned more toward running the ranch and breeding practices rather than the telling of fairy tales. "Something to write your travels in so you can remember them all when you come home."

Beau smiled, taking the journal from the young man who had grown to be the spitting image of Cyrus. There was no denying they were father and son. There was also no denying that Beau had always treated Johnny as if he were his own. He'd done that with his younger brothers as well—something both Cyrus and Cordell balked at more than once in their lives.

Now they were together to say goodbye—everyone except Cordell, his youngest brother. Cord had gotten married to a sweet woman who kept him in line and Beau thanked her for that. Sally Wilson had been exactly what Cordell needed in his life.

"I suppose Cordell is at the ranch?" Beau peered past Cyrus, hoping to see a cloud of dust being kicked up by an approaching rider. His heart sank slightly when there was none.

"He's doing the rounds. Said he'd catch up to you along the Brazos," Cyrus explained, taking a step closer to him, hesitation flickering in his eyes.

There was one thing the Kennedy men didn't do well—saying goodbye. In life or in death.

This may be the last time I see my family.

Beau lowered his head for a moment then pulled

Cyrus into a bear hug. "Take care of this family of yours."

"I will," Cyrus promised, holding Beau tight for a moment before stepping away from him. "Be careful and come home soon. The cabin is your home, as well as the ranch, when you're ready. And there'll be a new Kennedy for you to meet besides."

"I will." Beau tied his bags onto his saddle then turned to Johnny. "You better do me proud at university and don't get too used to the city. It will ruin you."

Johnny nodded then swiped his hand across his face. "I promise, Uncle Beau."

Beau took up his reins then mounted the patiently waiting gelding. "Tell Cordell …" Beau looked down at his brother, knowing no further words were needed. Beau would avoid running into Cordell at all costs, and by the look in his eyes, Cyrus knew it.

"We'll ride with you as far as—" Cyrus began, then stopped.

"No, we've said our goodbyes here. No sense in making it any longer than necessary." Beau settled into his saddle then rode northeast without looking back.

There was no reason to.

***

The air was thick and heavy, barely passable for breathing. The few sleeping passengers swayed softly to and fro in the stagecoach, completely unaware of what dangers may lay ahead of them. Only one kept watch. An unlikely soul with the eyes of an angel and the accuracy of a marksman.

Jessica Sanders would be grateful when the uncomfortable coach finally reached Brokengulch just over the Red River in Texas. Everything would be in place by now. She'd take up residence at The Cowboy Saloon and wait for her associate, whomever that may be, in the Sheldon case to make contact.

She didn't relish playing the saloon girl when a respectable schoolteacher assignment would have been more to her liking. Mr. Pinkerton had argued a good point, and she, for once, couldn't find fault with it. As a schoolteacher, she couldn't be seen at any of the less than respectable establishments Royce Sheldon might frequent. It wouldn't be proper for a teacher to be speaking with the likes of gamblers and others who found solace in the saloon. Whereas working in the saloon offered the perfect setting to obtain any news that would lead to his arrest.

She conceded and landed the part of Diamond LaRue to keep an eye out for Blue Eyes. According to the stream of Pinkerton informants, Royce Sheldon was reported to be making his way to Texas where rich ranch widows would be easy targets. She'd heard he could charm the stripes off a tigress then convince it to stroll into a lion's den without a second thought.

Jessica had gone over the file on Sheldon until it was embedded in her mind. Royce Sheldon, of Sheldon Banking & Loan in New York, had avoided prison and possibly death, thanks to his father's money and influence over the wealthy customers indebted to his bank. Sheldon had earned the name Blue Eyes due to their crystal color similar to the bluebell blooms in the spring, their beauty drawing in unsuspecting ladies. Any unfortunate woman who caught his eye fell under his spell, and so it was for Charlotte Henry, the young and beautiful wife of Judge Charles Henry of the New York Supreme Court.

According to the report, Judge Henry unexpectedly came home to find his wife straddled upon Sheldon's lap, completely bare-assed. The judge reported he'd dodged a bullet fired from Sheldon's Colt, but it had ricocheted and killed the judge's wife, the bullet penetrating her heart. Her bare breasts covered in crimson, she died in the judge's arms while Sheldon scampered half-dressed out the back door.

Sheldon fled the state in the dark of the night and disappeared for several years. That is, until word reached the judge a few months ago about a man matching Sheldon's description. Henry'd hired the Pinkerton Agency to bring Blue Eyes back for justice.

Jessica peered out the window for a moment then glanced back at her traveling companions. The young couple across from her dozed, their fingers entwined. The young lady's head nestled against her husband's shoulder, a small smile on her young face.

Justice. Where was her justice? A woman's broken heart should be able to find some sort of justice, shouldn't it?

If only this assignment hadn't brought her into Texas. What were the chances that she'd cross paths with that scoundrel Beau Kennedy? The day he walked away from her in the dead of the night some ten years earlier was as fresh now as it had been then.

Jess believed every word he'd ever written to her. Every promise he'd whispered in her ear those days they'd spent together in Dodge City. Everything about him was ingrained in her heart.

She'd never loved another. No man could take his place, no matter how much anguish Beau had caused her. He had left a scar on her heart forever with his scarlet letters and unfulfilled promises.

So why did her heart pound as they drew closer to Texas?

Why couldn't she shake his ghost from her life? His twinkling whiskey eyes haunted her at night when she fell asleep. His lips had branded hers with kisses as hot as fire. She was his, even if his brand couldn't be seen.

He'd left without an explanation other than a note

saying he cared for her deeply. That he was protecting her by leaving. That was the last she'd heard of him or his name.

Then she'd met Hollie Chandler and, under her guidance, became a Pinkerton operative. For many years, Jess would follow a lead on Beau only to find a dead end. There was no trace of a cowboy fitting his description; it was as if he'd disappeared. While Hollie understood Jessica's need to find him, she'd encouraged her to give up the cause. And five years ago she had.

But being this close to the land he loved brought it all back to her. And she didn't like it one bit.

The stage slowed. Jessica glanced out the window, and the ghost from her past faded back into the shadows. She smiled, her mind back on her assignment.

Brokengulch-5 Miles

"I'm coming for you, Blue Eyes," she whispered as the other passengers began to stir.

***

Beau rode into Brokengulch. Not much had changed since he'd last seen the error of his ways. He noted a newspaper office, *Gulch Reporter,* that hadn't been there before, tucked between the post office and Doc Clayton's office. The red-and-white-checkered curtains that hung in the sparkling clean windows of Miller's Cafe were new. A man ambled out the cafe door, digging around in his teeth with a toothpick and the look of a satisfied dog on his face. Either old Zeke Miller had died or his cooking had improved some because Beau remembered most people comparing Zeke's food to slop in a pig's trough. Down a few doors where Daisy's Jewels once stood was a bathhouse boasting everything from a shave to hot towels with personalized service upon request. Beau grinned, guessing what that "personalized service" entailed.

He reined his gelding up in front of The Gilded Lady, glancing up and down the street. The sooner he got to the bottom of this assignment, the better he'd like it. Even with its post office, newspaper, bustling businesses, and steeple-topped churches, something about Brokengulch still rattled him.

Pushing through the swinging doors, his holster low on his hip, the odor of stale cigar smoke crept over him. Beau quickly surveyed the room then moseyed up to the bar. There was a game of Faro going on in a corner, a bit tame for the place but suitable enough for the time of day. It was far too early for the girls to be seen on the floor even if it was nearly noon. A piano sat minding its own business along the wall next to the stage, resting from overexertion of the previous night. The place was nearly empty except for the card game and the man standing at the end of the bar, hat pulled down low on his head, seemingly buried in the drink sitting in front of him. He didn't fool Beau; the man knew exactly what was going on around him.

"What'll it be?" the bartender asked, wiping down the bar in front of Beau.

"Whiskey, straight up." Beau placed some coins in front of the barkeep then swigged down the gut warmer. "Where's the best place in town to bed down for a few nights?"

"Depends on what you're looking for. Rosie's can fix you up right pretty before you bed down somewhere." The barkeep gave him a wink and a toothy smile.

"Only looking for a place to put my head is about all," Beau smirked, pushing the empty glass toward the barkeep. The Gilded Lady may have cleaned up its facade, but Beau knew the danger lurking in its shadows. Past and present. "Thanks for the information on where to get a hot bath, though. I'll keep it in mind."

"The Conrad is the best if your pockets are deep enough." The man nodded, pouring Beau another two fingers of whiskey. "Otherwise there's The Rooster across the street. It's the oldest in town, but clean. Doesn't have the modern conveniences like The Conrad though. Nor the right kind of clientele."

"Thank ya kindly. I'll take that under advisement as well." Beau once more assessed the bartender, then walked across the sawdust-covered floor and out through the swinging doors. Brokengulch may have grown since he was last in town, but he could still smell trouble and this town was full of it. The chill creeping down his spine as he stood looking up and down the street confirmed his feeling.

The citizens ranged from the young, smart-looking woman in what Beau guessed to be latest fashion to the passing scruffy cowboy scratching his beard and giving off an odor that indicated he was in need of a hot bath. From the looks of his tattered clothes, he couldn't afford the personalized services of Rosie's Bathhouse. Children ran wild in the street dodging wagons and horses, screaming with delight.

He could almost smell the blood that had soaked the street long ago. Right or wrong, he'd contributed his share to the dirt and grime on more than one occasion. Beau hoped this time would be different; his wild days were long past him in more ways than one. It had been a while since he'd had to rely on his quickness with a gun.

Deciding to take up his temporary residence in The Rooster and visit an old friend, Beau crossed the rock-hard dirt street, each footfall feeling overwhelming familiar. He glanced up at the hotel sign, noting the wear and tear on the faded letters. The barkeep was correct in his assessment: The Rooster was the oldest hotel in town. Beau's gaze traveled down the row of second-floor windows to the last window in the east corner.

From there was the perfect view of anyone coming into town and of the Red River crossing to the north into Indian Territory.

His old room. After all these years, was it still his?

Beau pushed open the wooden door with its cracked etched window and a feeling of being home rushed over him. Nothing much had changed, including Mr. Carson. A bit older now, Carson still lorded over the registration desk as Beau remembered. Back then, not much got past Carson.

"Is 1D available?" Beau asked, doing his best to disguise his voice so Carson wouldn't know who he was.

"I'm sorry, but that room—" Carson looked from his work, a smile streaking across his face. "Why, Mr. Kennedy! When did you get back in town?"

"Long enough to have a whiskey at The Gilded Lady." Beau smiled, happy to see his old friend recognized him. "Last we saw each other, I believe you and Tilly were thinking of moving back East."

"Yes, well, after Tilly passed, I decided to stay here where I can be close to her." Carson came out from behind the desk, something Beau remembered he rarely, if ever, did. At least not so openly.

"I'm sorry to hear you lost her, Carson. She was a special woman." Beau shook the old man's hand, noting the fragility of it in his own. The determination in Carson's step was gone. Where was the vital man who'd been as quick with a gun as any gunslinger?

"She's buried on the hill with the boys." Carson's gaze turned to a place Beau had no business being in then returned in a flash. "I'll have your room ready and a bath drawn. Is there anything else, Mr. Kennedy?"

"Mr. Kennedy died long ago. It's Beau, Carson, and no, that'll be all," Beau said.

"Yes, sir." Carson smiled, snatching the key to 1D from the slot. He handed it across the desk then went back to his paperwork.

Beau took his key and started up the stairs.

"Welcome back, Beau."

Carson's soft words trailed up the steps after him.

CHAPTER TWO

The stagecoach bounced into town, hitting every ripple in the road. Jessica spied Rosie's Bathhouse, her body groaning in response to the words "hot bath" painted across the storefront. A fancy hotel they passed produced a longing that The Conrad would be where she'd lay her head, but she knew differently. It was far too rich looking for the likes of Diamond LaRue. The driver finally stopped in front of a saloon called The Gilded Lady. Jessica wondered if her assignment had been correct. She'd not seen another establishment of drink and entertainment in town. Where was The Cowboy Saloon? Was there such an establishment? Or had the information been wrong? It wouldn't be the first time the wrong intelligence had been passed along to the Pinkerton Detective Agency office.

The stagecoach door swung open. Jessica slid across the seat then disembarked, leaving the two lovebirds behind. At least she wouldn't be subjected to their affections any longer. She'd learned long ago to never trust the heart. Looking around, Jessica took a deep breath then accepted her large carpet valise from the driver. Without further haste, the man climbed back onto the box, snapping the team into motion.

"Goodbye, Jessica Sanders. Hello, Diamond LaRue," Jessica said under her breath, stepping up onto the boardwalk in front of The Gilded Lady. She'd been instructed to go to The Cowboy and ask for Miss Layla Lyons, but she had to find it first.

Strolling down the walkway, Jessica stopped in at Rosie's for directions and to begin scoping out the town's people for an ally, if needed. A young blond-haired woman from behind the counter looked up as the bell tinkled. The woman's smile was warm and inviting, but her young face held lines around a pair of weary brown eyes. The scent of lavender and roses overwhelmed the room, sickeningly so, as far as Jessica was concerned.

"I'm sorry, we're all full up right now."

"Oh, that's fine. I'm looking for The Cowboy Saloon. Can you tell me where I might find it?" Jessica smiled, thankful she couldn't be tempted for that hot bath she longed for. It would only delay her arrival at her post anyway. Besides, she wanted to get on with the business at hand as quickly as possible.

"Yes, ma'am. Keep going down the walkway and around the bend. It sits between the Cumberland Bank and Lane's Livery."

"Thank you, Miss—" Jessica smiled, hoping she'd made her first *friend* in Brokengulch.

"Lucie Pletcher," Lucie said, her eyes reflecting her thankfulness for the courtesy, something Jessica felt sure the girl heard little of.

"Lucie, I am thankful for your help. I'm Diamond LaRue, new in town and looking for—" Jessica began.

"Miss Layla, I would guess," Lucie said, the friendly smile fading from her face. "You'll find her at The Cowboy this time of day, getting her girls ready for tonight. Or at least attempting to."

"Wonderful! Thank you again, Lucie." Jessica strolled over to the door then turned as her hand grasped the knob. "I hope to see you soon, Lucie. Take care."

"Yes, ma'am," Lucie replied as she turned back to her books.

Jessica stepped out onto the boardwalk and glanced

around, getting the layout of the town. Across the street was the sheriff's office and the mercantile, which she'd need sooner or later, she was sure. A painted sign on the building next door indicated the town's doctor. The church steeple jutted into the sky above the rooftops like a beacon of goodness.

At least there is a place of worship in town, one where the sins of the week can be repented. Jessica strolled pass the office of the *Gulch Reporter* then dodged a man rushing out of the land office with a grudge firmly planted on his shoulders. *Well, he's unhappy about something!*

Rounding the corner, across from the school where the Cumberland Bank stood, Jessica spied her destination—The Cowboy Saloon and Dance Hall. Straightening her shoulders, she took a step forward. Her hips swaying in exaggeration, she pushed through the doors as Diamond LaRue.

"May I help you?" A man sporting a well-trimmed beard and round glasses approached her. His clothing was pressed, clean, and of the latest fashion she'd last seen in Boston before embarking on her assignment. This had to be Lute North, manager of The Cowboy; but that was all she knew about the man—for now.

"Yes, I'm looking for Miss Layla Lyons," Jessica replied, patting her hair and batting her eyes.

"I'm Layla Lyons."

Jessica looked up. A regal woman with light red hair piled neatly on her head stood at the top of the steps. Her high-collared, deep purple dress captured the light that came through the door. Satin, guessed Jessica, as the woman gazed pointedly at her.

A woman of power, or so she thinks. Well, we shall see.

"Miss Lyons, I am Diamond LaRue. I believe you have been expecting me." Turning on her best Boston accent, Jessica introduced herself, nodding slightly.

"Yes, of course. Miss LaRue, you may come upstairs, and we will get you settled. Lute, have a tray sent to my room for Miss LaRue, please," Layla instructed, her position not wavering once. "And a hot bath drawn as well."

"Right away, Miss Layla." Lute glanced at Jessica, his eyes raking her from head to toe. Then he disappeared into a back room once he was satisfied with his assessment of her.

Jessica smiled as she proceeded up the stairs, leaving behind any lingering remnants of her real self.

"Right this way, Miss LaRue." Layla Lyons appeared to be a woman of breeding, or one who longed to be at the very least. Boston society, if her manner of speaking were true. The light, crisp scent of white roses reminded Diamond of her mother.

Layla Lyons didn't seem the motherly type with her rigid back and stiff manner.

Diamond followed, noting each of the room doors were closed. It was quiet, unsettlingly so. It was nearly noon. Where was everyone?

"I understand that you are well versed in the waltz, Miss LaRue. It is a dance that is lacking in my dance hall. The other girls aren't sufficiently adept at the steps and cannot lead our patrons very well." Layla pushed open the door to the room at the end of the shadowed hall. "Please do come in. Lute will have refreshments here in a moment."

Diamond stepped into the large, elegantly furnished room. A deep royal blue parlor set sat near the window draped in matching velvet and lace curtains. A carved table sat on a Persian rug in front of the settee with a crystal vase filled with prairie flowers on it. Along the outside wall was an ornate fireplace empty of any soot or signs of recent use. Two side chairs with heart-shaped cushioned backs flanked the matching settee. The carved, dark wood gleamed with a high polish. Diamond recognized the Eastlake style and made a mental note that Layla Lyons may indeed be a wealthy woman. The kind of wealth that came from more than running a dance hall in the middle of a small Texas town.

"Miss LaRue, sadly I recently lost one of my best girls. Based on your inquiry, I am willing to offer you a position here starting immediately. However, there are a few rules that you must abide by. Disregard for them will not be tolerated." Layla sat in the middle of the settee then motioned for Diamond to sit in one of the other chairs.

"You must understand the importance that I maintain the appearance of a respectable establishment. I do not openly offer companionship to our customers, other than a dance." A tap at the door brought the conversation to a halt. "Yes, Lute, please do come in."

Lute entered, carrying a silver tray supporting a teapot, two cups, and a few finger sandwiches. Diamond smiled up at the man, whose eyes were glued on Layla.

"Lute, this is Miss Diamond LaRue. She will be starting tonight, so please be sure to have a waltz or two ready as her introduction to our best customers. And please check on the bath being drawn for Miss Diamond; she's had a long journey and is in need of one. All those long hours riding in a stagecoach can be so wearisome."

"As you wish, Miss Layla." Lute smiled, winked, then left the room whistling a tune, his manner easy and unassuming. Quite different from the man Diamond had met when she'd first arrived. Was he afraid of Layla? Or just lusted after her?

"Now, Miss LaRue, I have a room ready for you. I ask no questions of my girls' pasts. It doesn't matter to me. You are to keep your dance card filled, flirt but nothing more." Layla poured them each a cup of tea with the grace of an educated woman, then motioned for Jessica to help herself to a sandwich. "Above all else be respectable in your manner. Your customer is never to believe you are offering more than that dance. If he does, please send him to me and I will handle the arrangements. Are there any questions, Miss LaRue?"

"No, Miss Lyons, you have made everything perfectly clear. And I fully understand my obligations to you and the customers." Diamond smiled, setting her tea down next to her partially eaten sandwich.

"Good! Now then." Layla rose, her hands clasped in front of her. "Let's get you settled. Your bath should be waiting for you by now."

Layla turned on her heel and walked briskly across the room. Diamond snapped to follow her. No sense giving Layla Lyons any reason to think she had no control over Diamond LaRue.

"You will be staying in room 3B. There isn't a wonderful view of the river and trees. Instead, you'll have the noise from the street. Some nights you won't get your proper rest until you've grown used to it." Layla opened the door then stepped aside as Diamond crossed the threshold. "There are several dresses in the wardrobe for you to try. Once you have found a few that fit, please give the rest to Lute. Be downstairs by six o'clock."

Diamond nodded then looked around her room. A functional bed with clean sheets, two pillows, and a plain-colored blanket. The single window was framed with dark curtains. A washbowl and pitcher sat on the dresser next to the one chair and small table. The steaming copper tub sat in the middle of the room, beckoning her. She closed the door, turning the lock.

For at least an hour she'd have peace of mind before a quick nap and then dance into the hearts of those she needed to befriend.

***

Beau strolled out onto the street, aware of the sun setting in the west. The girls who'd found their way onto the balcony of The Gilded Lady were advertising their available services. The town's scent and feel changed as it transitioned from day into night. Instead of dirt and horses and leather, it became smoky. Gritty. Dangerous.

Beau wondered if The Cowboy would be a perfect match to the hum of the town, and it wasn't so far he couldn't walk it. If it were earlier, he might have considered a leisurely stroll through Brokengulch and the chance to become reacquainted with the town. Now that night was falling, he decided to ride his gelding just in case he—well, just in case. He felt more in control for some reason.

Just like the Peacemaker on his hip made him feel the same. That's where his true control lay—in his quick and true aim. Beau realized long ago the only things he could depend on were his wits and his gun. Always there, waiting for his attention, giving back each and every time. Maybe the old bounty hunter traits were surfacing.

Had they ever really left?

In the years since he'd rode away from the brutal life of a bounty hunter, the .45 had seen little use. There had been no real need—until now. Beau felt useful again; that itch was finally being scratched. The other he ignored to the best of his ability, except at night when his dreams reminded him of what could have been his.

The bouncy notes of *Camptown Races* filtering out onto the street sparked the ghost of a certain dark-haired beauty in his arms. Regret was a hard pill to swallow; for Beau, this was one lodged in his throat forever. The sounds of a few men singing along with the gay tune reminded him further of those happier times. He'd been foolish enough to believe he was good enough for the woman he loved. All he was good at was knowing that the loud men were the beginnings of what was sure to be a bawdy night.

Pushing through the swinging doors, Beau stepped up to the bar and ordered a whiskey straight up. The music switched abruptly to a waltz. A sea of whistles followed by hoots and hollers roused his curiosity enough to look up. A woman walked slowly down the stairs. Piercing blue eyes darted back and forth over the small crowd of admirers gathering on the dance floor. A ruby red smile graced her lips, lighting up her perfect porcelain face. Red feathers accented her coal-black hair. The red dress hugged her curves like a second skin.

Curves Beau was all too familiar with.

What the hell is she doing here? Every muscle in his body quivered with the urge to run up the stairs, drag her into a room, and have his way with her. Then put Jessica Sanders over his knee and give her a right proper spanking for dressing the way she was.

"Gentlemen, I am pleased to introduce you to Miss Diamond LaRue," the red-haired woman standing just behind Jessica announced, her head cocked slightly toward Jessica. "Miss Diamond will be filling her card tonight. Her specialty is the waltz, but she will be dancing all night, so please line up to add your name to her card. If you don't know the waltz, Miss LaRue will instruct you. And remember, one at a time or you'll have to answer to me!"

"Yes ma'am, Miss Layla!" The gawking men answered in a chorus.

Diamond LaRue? Beau watched on as one after another, the men scribbled their mark on the dance card. A surge of jealously gripped at his soul. He had no right to Jessica. So why was he feeling like he should punish her with a good paddling, dressed as she was?

Jessica smiled sweetly, watching with interest as the

card passed from one man to another until the crowd finally thinned. Head down, Beau stepped forward when the last name was scribbled down.

"Mind if I add my name to that dance card?"

"Of course not." Diamond passed the card and pencil over then looked up. Her blue eyes widened. Her face grew pale and her mouth gaped open.

"Thank you, Miss *Diamond*!" Beau scrawled his name on the bottom of the list. "I'd close that pretty little mouth of yours before someone asks any questions." Looking up into her eyes, he handed the card back, tipped his hat, then walked away.

"All right, that's it, boys. Miss Diamond will be back later," Miss Layla said, turning her newest girl back to the stairs. "Rosie's has room for anyone who is willing to smell sweeter than a sow."

Beau ordered another whiskey, downing it in one gulp as he watched the woman who held his heart walk back up the stairs dressed looking like a soiled dove.

No! It can't be. Jessica trailed up the steps behind Miss Layla. She glanced down at her card, then quickly over to the bar, confirming Beau Kennedy had indeed written his name down. She hadn't been hallucinating after all. *Why, after all these years?*

"Appears you'll be occupied all night, Miss LaRue. If I were you, I'd get a bit of rest over the next hour," Layla suggested, leaving Jessica standing at the door to her small but functional room.

How was she going to do her job with that scoundrel Beau Kennedy lurking around? Hands on her hips, Jessica paced around the room.

"Why after all these years has that scalawag suddenly shown up?" Jess plopped down across the bed and stared up at the cracked ceiling. The last person she wanted back in her life, even if only for a dance, was

Beauregard Kennedy. A deep wrinkle a hot iron couldn't take care of. She didn't owe him any explanation. She wasn't the one at fault.

"He's the last dance of the night," Jessica thought out loud. "Dance with him. Say goodbye and be rid of him. It's as easy as that. No problem."

Satisfied with her decision, Jessica freshened up then changed into a royal blue and black satin dress that fell just above her knees in the front and inches above the floor in the back. She smoothed the black stockings up her calves and over her knees, then put on her shoes, lacing them up just pass her ankles.

Twisting a curl back into her long, black hair Jessica slipped a silver comb into a tendril of hair behind her ear. The silver setting glimmered against the dark strands. Hopefully tonight she'd find out if her Pinkerton contact had signed her dance card.

The sooner that happened, the sooner she could find and arrest Royce Sheldon, then get back to her life and onto the next assignment.

"Let's go, girls!" Miss Layla sang out, knocking on Jessica's door as she marched down the hall. "These men aren't going to wait all night to dance with you."

Jessica drew a breath then walked out of her room, following several women of different ages down the stairs. She glanced around the saloon. Her heart sank with disappointment; Beau wasn't anywhere in sight.

The piano rang out *Oh Suzanna* loud and clear. Each of the girls grabbed their dance partners as a chorus of laughter filled the saloon. Jessica scanned each face, but not one of the men in attendance matched the description she'd been given of Royce Sheldon.

I got here ahead of him. Good. Jessica continued down the stairs then found a spot near the piano. The girls were laughing and seemed to be having fun. The men were either dancing or drinking or playing cards at one of the tables.

"You should have let me know you were coming, darling." Miss Layla's typically stern and no-nonsense voice was now sing-songish and flirty with the man in front of her. She linked her arm through his, a hand stroking the front of his shirt. "I would have made sure the new girl saved a waltz for you. As it is, Miss Diamond's card filled up rather quickly but if you desire, I can arrange an opening on one of the dance cards. Maybe Miss Alice. Or, if you insist, Miss Diamond, my new girl?"

Jessica ducked behind a post close to the piano. Blond hair. Mustache. Beautiful blue eyes a female could swim in. Pretty boy looks. Yes, that was Royce Sheldon. What was Layla doing talking to him? They looked pretty friendly for it to be only a business acquaintance. Why was she so chummy with the wanted man?

This just became more than an apprehend and arrest assignment.

"You always take good care of me, Layla. I'll have to defer dancing for another night though. I'm more in the mood for a few drinks up at the bar. I'll see you in the morning." Sheldon kissed Layla on the cheek then walked away from the woman, calling over his shoulder. "You know where I am staying while in town."

Miss Layla smiled then turned her attention back to dancers with scrutiny. She glided over to the man at the piano, whispered in his ear, and the music switched from a quick step to a waltz without skipping a beat.

Jessica stepped out from the shadow and into the arms of the first man on her dance card. Red Calhoun was an older gentleman who smelled like rotting roses. No amount of bathing over at Rosie's had put a dent into his stale body odor. His hair was slicked back in a cap of gray streaked with ginger.

The music finished. Jessica smiled, thanked Mr. Calhoun, then walked away from the man, inhaling deeply. Turning, she slipped into the arms of Beau.

He pulled her close, twirling her around the room to the strains of *Oh, My Darling Clementine*. The woodsy smell of his body invoked familiar memories of their few glorious months together. A quick courtship filled with love, romance, and promises.

Unfulfilled promises.

"What the hell are you doing here, Jess?" Beau hissed in a whisper, his eyes holding her gaze.

She shivered, the heat scorching her through and through, before she looked away from his accusing eyes. "Dancing." Not daring to look up into his face again, she kept her focus over his shoulder and on the passing faces. "Why do you care?"

"Because you shouldn't be here," Beau hissed, his body tensing against her. "Go back to your life in Boston before your father comes to get you again."

Jessica fought back the tears threatening, forcing a smile on her face. "Daddy doesn't control me anymore. I control what I do now, Mr. Kennedy."

"Really? Since when?" If at all possible, he pulled her closer; his breath hot ice against her skin.

"Since you walked out of my life," she replied, the music switching back to a waltz. "Thank you for the dance, sir. I have another partner waiting his turn."

For more information or to keep on reading to find out if Jessica gets her man, or if she loses her heart to Beau, please visit https://bit.ly/2OKASh0

Red River Crossing is available in ebook, print, and audio at all book retailer sites.

ABOUT THE AUTHOR

Maxine Douglas first began writing in the early 1970s while in high school. She took every creative writing course offered at the time and focused her energy for many years after that on poetry. It wasn't until a dear friend's sister revealed she was about to become a published author that jumpstarted Maxine into getting the ball rolling; she finished her first manuscript in a month's time.

Maxine Douglas and her late husband moved to Oklahoma in 2010 from Wisconsin. Since then Maxine has rekindled her childhood love of westerns. She has four children, two granddaughters, her first great grandbaby in 2021, and a shelter kitty named Simon. And many friends she now considers her Oklahoma family.

One of the things Maxine has learned over the years is that you can never stop dreaming and reaching for the stars. Sooner or later you touch one and it'll bring you more happiness than you can ever imagine. Maxine feels lucky, and blessed, that over the past several years she's been able to reach out and touch the stars--and she's still reaching.

Maxine loves to hear from her readers. So, come on by and say "Hello"; Maxine would love to hear from you.

You can catch her on:

Facebook Reader Group:
https://www.facebook.com/groups/maxinesbookdivas/
X (fka Twitter): https://x.com/waMaxineDouglas
TikTok: https://tiktok.com/@maxinedouglasauthor
Goodreads:
https://www.goodreads.com/author/show/6423715.Maxine_Douglas
BookBub: https://www.bookbub.com/authors/maxine-douglas